GRIMOIRE
ANTHOLOGY

VOLUME I
DARK MIRROR

Destiny Universe Created by Bungie

To our community,
You've become the main characters in the stories we tell.
You've filled our worlds with your light and your friendship.
Thank you for your passion for our games and for each other.
Most of all, thank you for playing.

foreword

The stories tell of a golden age, long ago, when our civilization spanned the system. It was a bright and hopeful time, but it didn't last...

With these few words, the first delicate seeds of a universe were sown. Many hands had already begun to nurture the primordial ideas and form the bedrock of a world; many, many more would soon come to lend themselves to the task of tending what would become vast and varied gardens of story, and of names and places springing forth from the fundament. Some grew and grasped for the light, blossomed, and as human creations so often do, many of our world's myths and monuments fell to ruin.

And now, here you are in the midst of a thousand radiant roses and ruinous ends. Within this anthology is a selection of voices—the fictional, but very much living characters that have witnessed the collapse of an age, yet goad and strive to shape a future to their own design.

These tales, too, are only just a beginning. As you read, you may detect a thousand more stories still to come, dormant, hidden deep within the fertile soil. They'll whisper and grasp and dare to take root in your imagination—to inspire you not only with what is revealed and implied by these words, these pages, these works, but to allow you to imagine what may yet emerge. Each new revelation may itself be a seed to sow, nurture, and tend in the shaping of worlds to come.

introduction

I have always felt that this world contains secrets, forgotten stories waiting to be discovered. However, like many players, I first ignored that feeling, and just pursued precious loot. It was only after my vault was full, and my enemies defeated that I asked why; why am I doing this?

So it began. I read the journals of defeated enemies, the memories of a dying Ghost, the etchings on the barrel of a weapon, and realized there was much more to this world. I became not only a player but a storyteller, a chronicler of *Destiny*'s history, infusing my discoveries with my own perspectives and interpretations. Weapons were no longer just weapons, armor no longer just armor, and enemies no longer just targets. Understanding the lore of *Destiny* complemented and enhanced the gameplay. Pulling the trigger now had weight, rockets howled with the sacrifice of fallen Guardians.

I was not the first, and I will not be the last. Many others have been inspired by the history and fiction of *Destiny*, piecing together fragments of the *Destiny* Universe in their own way. Some stories are hidden, misleading, deceptive, and still fiercely debated. This anthology does not set out to solve these disputes but, instead, entice you to join the conversation.

Destiny Grimoire Anthology, Volume I: Dark Mirror, is about your path as a Guardian and the haunting temptation of the dark. The collection of lore entries that follows challenges you to see this world through different perspectives: the vanquished, the corrupted, and the shattered. It does not represent everything, but rather presents a version of events told by many characters, through many eyes.

The truth is for you to decide.

From,

A fellow Guardian

DARK MIRROR

CHAPTER 1

A Book of Sorrow

What is this violent ritual? These tales of suffering, where all ends in a feast of maggots and rot laid on a wormwood table for gods to feast on misery?

But is not the Light also served by savage sacrifice? Accepted wounds? Blood spilled on the dust of distant worlds?

Life and death and life and death and life and death are locked in a battle that never ends.

The cycle is the same. The pain is the same. We eliminate those who oppose the Light. They annihilate those who do not worship the Dark.

In the end, only sorrow remains.

Verse 1:0
The Fundament

Dearest sister,

It's taken me two years—a quarter of our lives—but I've found the proof. We aren't native to the Fundament. Our ancient ancestors came here to hide.

The plate of stone we live on, our Osmium Court, is one fragment of a rocky planet that crashed into the Fundament and broke apart. All the other nearby continents— the Helium Drinkers, the Bone Plaza, the Starcutters—came from the same world.

Perhaps the other races of the Fundament are migrants too.

We live on the shrapnel of our homeworld, floating on an ocean deep inside a gas giant.

That's what Fundament must be. A titanic gas planet. The endless storm above us must be one layer of the atmosphere. And the sea we float on... there's more down beneath it. So much more!

You understand what this means, Sathona. The Timid Truth is a lie. We aren't meant to be the world's prey. We weren't born to live and die in the dark.

We have a better destiny.

Tell our father, sister Sathona. This is the proof of his life's work.

With love, for your second birthday,
Your first surviving sister,
Aurash

Verse 1:1
Predators

Predators and Menaces —
Carved to endure by Xi Ro —
Third surviving sister of the Osmium King's last brood —

A STORMJOY. A stormjoy is a living cloud. When it passes over our continent, it lowers its feeding tentacles. On each tentacle are the BAIT STARS. Although light makes you happy, you must avoid it. You will be eaten.

A stormjoy is a good way for an old person to choose death. Also, a daring knight can cut the bait stars from the tentacles. I have six!

FALLING. If you fall off the edge of the continent, you will die in the ocean! This is a special hazard when our father the Osmium King uses the engines.

HELIUM DRINKERS. The currents of the Fundament Ocean bring us near other continents. The Helium Court is near us now. They are of our species, but they are our enemies. Their knights raid us every day. Helium Drinkers have two legs, two arms, and three eyes, just like us. But they are bright/evil. I want to be a knight and fight them!

The Helium Drinker ambassador ate ten of my sisters as tribute. This is normal. However, I resent it.

MOTHERS. Mothers can fly! They live much longer than ten years. Mothers are extremely smart, and they guard their spawn. If you try to tamper with the eggs, they will eat you. Sathona wants to eat the jelly and become a mother when she turns four.

STORMS. The rain is often poisonous. Sometimes it dissolves flesh. When lightning misses the lightning farm, it can vaporize a person.

This entire world is deadly to us.

MYSTERIES. The Fundament is very large. We are the smallest things in it. If you don't understand something, it will probably kill you. My teacher Taox says this is why we have such short lives. So we can breed and adapt quickly.

MOON WAVES. My sister Aurash is afraid of moon waves. When she gets back from her expedition to the Tungsten Monoliths, I will ask her why.

Verse 1:2
The Hateful Verse

For the consideration of the Helium Court,
Written in desperation,
This sealed secret,

I am Taox, sterile mother, teacher to the children of the Osmium Throne.

As a mother, I live long. As a neuter, I can rise above the small battles of court politics.

I alone see the patterns of survival. Alone I designed the great engines that move the Osmium Court. Now—

Alone I must act to save my kingdom.

Senility has claimed my lord the Osmium King. He is ten, and mad. The study of ancient text consumes him. Today he raves about moons above the storm. Tomorrow he will wander the halls, speaking to his familiar, a dead white worm from the deep sea. He keeps it in glass, and he tends to it, and he neglects the duties of a king.

The Osmium King has three surviving heirs, each two years old:

Xi Ro, the youngest and bravest, who wants to be a knight.

Sathona, most clever, who wants to be a mother.

Aurash, navigator child, who dreams of the infinite ocean. Tomorrow she will return from the Tungsten Monoliths.

None of these are suitable heirs. None of them will protect the Osmium Court from the howling Fundament. Xi Ro can fight, but not lead. Sathona can think, but not fight. Aurash's curiosity will draw her away from duty. I fear for all future children.

Soon the Osmium King will lock himself into the Royal Orrery to study the moons. Gather your knights, o Helium Drinkers, and invade our continent. Kill the three heirs. I will rule the Osmium Court as your regent, and build engines for you.

And if I fail, let the Leviathan in the deep eat me.

Written in grief,
This hateful request,
Taox, Osmium-mother, neutered to watch

Verse 1:3

The Oath

Sisters! This is how an oath is done. Put your left hands on the mast, close to mine.

Take the knife in your right hand. Push it through your left hand, straight between the bones. Now! Carve a blood line down the mast.

Speak your oath.

"I am Xi Ro, youngest daughter of the dead king. I will take back my Osmium Court and kill the traitor Taox. On my left eye I swear vengeance."

In blood the oath is made.

"I am Sathona, middle daughter of the dead king. I will take back my home and eat the mother jelly. I will raise my spawn on the corpse of the Helium King. On my right eye I promise this."

In blood the oath is made.

Now...

"I will help make your oath, sister."

"I will help it too."

I am Aurash, first daughter of the dead king. I will chase my father's last screamed warning. I will know what changed the motion of our moons. If the end of the world is coming, I will understand why.

On my center eye I swear it. I will understand.

"In blood the oath is made."

"In blood."

Thank you, sisters. We have only my ship left to us. But a ship is freedom! We have secrets to hunt, storm-lit realms to explore, and great armies to raise.

Put up the lightning sails, and we will voyage far.

Verse 1:4

Syzygy

The Syzygy —
Carved to endure by Aurash —
The high vengeance —

Only Xi Ro's bait stars let us escape. Only Sathona's tricks let us reach the coast. But now that we have my ship, I must lead the way. I am the navigator.

We may never see our homes again. Xi Ro seethes with hate and fury for Taox.

But this is my deepest fear—

Our civilization drifts on the Fundament. At the Tungsten Monoliths I learned that thousands of other species drift with us, coexisting on a vast world sea. And the tides of the Fundament move us all.

The Timid Truth says that we are the smallest, most fragile things alive. The natural prey of the universe. Taox would have us believe that our ancestors came to the Fundament to hide from the hungry void.

My father died afraid. Not of vile Taox or the Helium Drinkers, but of his orrery. He screamed to me—

"Aurash, my first daughter! The moons are different! The laws are bent!"

And he made the sign of a syzygy.

Imagine the fifty-two moons of Fundament lining up in the sky. (It wouldn't take all fifty-two, of course: just a few massive moons. But this is my deepest fear.) Imagine their gravity pulling on the Fundament sea, lifting it into a swollen bulge...

Imagine that bulge collapsing as the syzygy passed. A wave big enough to swallow civilizations. A God-Wave.

I have to find a way to stop it. Before the God-Wave annihilates my species. If I could only get back into my father's orrery, I could learn exactly when!

We are weeks of travel and many continents away from home.

When I'm paralyzed by fear, Xi Ro sits in the cabin with me and comforts me with soft, brave words. But more and more we have come to rely on Sathona's wit. She will go off to be alone (she insists she must be alone) and return with some mad idea—steer into the storm, throw down a net, eat that strange beast, explore that menacing wreck.

Somehow Sathona seems to manufacture good luck by sheer will.

Verse 1:5
Needle and Worm

My secrets —
Carved in my code by Sathona —
The right eye vengeance —

1. This year of wild voyaging, these lightning nights and golden days, these forays into ancient wrecks and windblown flights from monsters: these are the happiest times of my life.

2. I want to be a mother not because I want to spawn but because I want a long life. Long enough to make a difference. We have been at sea a year and I am afraid, afraid we will die out here.

3. I know where to find secrets. I know where vast slow things with long memories live.

4. The needle ship…

The needle ship —
Carved in my code by Sathona —
A liar —

1. We salvaged the needle from the Shvubi Maelstrom. I knew it would be there.

2. The needle is a gray ship, as long and slender as hope, as unbreakable as time, and old. Older than death. It tumbled through the maelstrom before our ancestors crashed into the Fundament. This is not a sea-ship, like Aurash's. It is an artifact of high technology.

3. I know its purpose. I know what happened to the crew.

4. Xi Ro wants to sell the ship at Kaharn Atoll, where species gather. At auction, it would earn us enough wealth to hire mercenaries. We could retake our Osmium Court and send the baby-eating Helium Drinkers screaming into the ocean—

5. —but I told Xi Ro the ship was worthless.

6. Aurash wants to open the ship and see if we can take command of it. I know this is the right thing to do. I know because I asked the worm...

The worm —
Carved in my code by Sathona —
Who should be afraid —

1. It was my father's familiar. I ripped it from him as we fled. It is a dead white thing, segmented, washed up from the deep sea.

2. It's dead, but it still speaks to me. It says: listen closely, oh vengeance mine...

Verse 1:6

Sisters

A register of tokens and gestures exchanged before the end of sisterhood.

"Xi Ro, my brave sister, you have worked too hard to move the carcasses out of the birthing room! Come. Steer the ship for a while. Take joy in what our needle can do."

Xi Ro tried to protest, but secretly, she was so glad for Aurash's care. She flew the needle ship in cutting circles, down beneath the sea: and their wake rose up to the surface like a traitor's dying breath.

"Aurash, lonely navigator, we have traveled so long with only each other. I know you love to hear and speak new tongues. Come, sit in the flesh garden room. I will read you these stories I bought at Kaharn."

Aurash sat among the mummified flesh fans with two of her eyes closed and listened in silence to Sathona's stories, hungry to understand, voracious to know as much as she could before her ten year life died.

Later, Xi Ro said, "Sathona, cutting mind of ours, you grow lonely in your thought. Play swords and lanterns with me!"

But Sathona was heavy with sorrow, and couldn't pretend any joy as she chased Xi Ro through the needle's glistening halls.

"Sathona, pensive one, what is it? What troubles you?"

Her sisters listened as Sathona said "Oath-bearing siblings, we are five years old. For two years we've worked to repair this ancient ship and understand its systems. I am almost too old for the mother jelly, and the knights who killed our father are surely dying of age.

"We three will die here, in exile. Taox will outlive us. And Aurash, brilliant-eyed Aurash, you will die of old age long before you have proof of your God-Wave, or any way to stop it."

Aurash and Xi Ro looked at each other. "I wish you weren't so honest," Xi Ro said. And Aurash thought that Sathona had never been wrong.

In her soul Aurash knew that the only way to keep their oath was to find a great, powerful secret. A secret that could change everything. This was Aurash's soul, her fire and her shadow—her desire to cut through the flank of the world and find its beating heart.

"We have to dive," Aurash said. "That's what this ship is built to do. Dive into the Fundament, the world below us... towards the core."

"That's where the ancient crew died so obscenely," Xi Ro protested. "That's where the atrocity in the birthing room was born..."

"We have to dive," Sathona said, following the whispers of her familiar. "In the world beneath us, in the metallic depths, I hope we may find what we need most..."

More time. More life.

Verse 1:7
The Dive

For life, Sathona dove. For vengeance, Xi Ro dove. And Aurash dove to understand.

The needle ship pierced the skin of the world and burrowed deep. Through layers of foam and metal and cold elemental slush. Aurash devoured the ship's maps of Fundament, from the high angelic cloud decks, down and down through storms and oceans and plates of floating world, into the crush of the core.

They met monsters of continental scope. Vast anemones that raised glowing tentacles to bait them in. Xi Ro flew the needle ship through them and they bled black carbon jelly and frost.

They came to a still place, beneath a plate of metal.

"I'll use the sensors," whispered Aurash. "Listen..."

In the wet gold dark of the helm, they listened to the ship, and the ship listened to the crushing motions of Fundament.

They heard the collision of continents. They heard the patter and the crash of helium-neon rain. They heard the struggles of monsters. And they heard the distant groan of the ocean rising. Tugged by distant moons.

"The syzygy is real..." Sathona hissed. "It's already begun."

Behind them, Xi Ro thought of the birthing-room, where ancient explorers had labored over surgeries and administrations, peeling back the chrysalis and the caul of that which they had made from the deep, whose birth none of them would survive...

"There's something down here," she whispered. "Something secret."

And the Leviathan loomed over them, its brow as huge all the continents of their childhood, its great array-fins crackling with the lightning of its life. Booming into the hull of the needle ship in a microwave voice:

++YOU MUST TURN BACK—
—SAVE YOURSELVES FROM THE DEEP++
++SAVE THE WORLD FROM YOURSELVES—
—YOU MUST TURN BACK++

Verse 1:8

Leviathan

The Leviathan's Warning

++We live on the edge of a war—
—a war between Formless and Form++
++between the Deep and the Sky—

++MY EYES ARE WIDE, MY GAZE IS LONG++

—Across the universe, as far as I see++
++the Sky works to charge its fires—
—and the Deep drowns the ash++

—Sky builds gentle places, safe for life++
++Beloved Fundament, refuge of trillions—
—The Sky treasures this rich place++

—BUT THE DEEP IS HERE WITH US—

++Cold logic tests our walls—
—The Deep claims its dominion++
++A ruthless, final age —

Aurash's Protest

Old Leviathan, creature of myth, this world is no refuge. We live short, hard lives. We die in the dark. The storm above us will never end. And soon the God-Wave will take us all. Above us there are only stormjoys, monsters, and moons of apocalypse. Let us go down, down, where we may discover truth, some power to avenge ourselves upon our betrayers, some hope of survival.

The Leviathan's Hope

—What power calls you++
++Down to the deep?—

++What instinct draws you—
—Away from high hope?++

—Quick-breeding krill people, I tell you++
++For eons I have watched your struggle—
—Clinging to the sharp edge of survival++
++Balanced between the Deep and the Sky.—

++You were my treasure—
—My proof against despair++

—FOR THIS IS THE DEEP CLAIM—

++Existence is the struggle to exist—
—When the struggle seems lost++
++when the safe place crumbles—
—everything turns to the Deep to survive++

++I REJECT THE DEEP CLAIM++

—You will turn back, sweet krill of hope.±±
++You will choose the Sky instead.—

Xi Ro's Protest

You are huge and old! Our lives are short and desperate. If that's the way the world's supposed to be, I won't have it! If people like Taox are supposed to win, I won't let them! I'll beat the world until it changes! I'll kill anything in the way!

The Leviathan's Dirge

++This fatal logic++
—Hear my monopole scream!—
++It will consume you++

—Before you lies—
++The worship of death++
—The ruinous path—

++The Sky builds new life++
—Against the onset of ruin—
++Towards a gentle world++

—The Deep embraces death—
++Saying: this is inevitable and right++
—I exist as hungry ruin—

++TURN BACK FROM THE WORLD-KILLING WAY++
++OR YOU WILL LIVE AS DEATH AND DEVASTATION++
—The Sky is the harder way. But it is kinder.—
—My charge is balanced: my voice exhausted.—

Sathona's Protest

Sisters, I have my father's familiar. Look! It answers me in plain words. It helped me find this ship. It gives me strength when hope is lost.

Who will you trust? The voice that wants us to live and suffer, as we have lived and suffered? The Leviathan that offers no hope against Taox or the world-wave?

Or the plain, honest worm?

Let us see where its whisper leads us, Aurash. Let us go deeper, Xi Ro!

Let us dive, oh sisters mine.

Verse 1:9
The Bargain

You are Aurash. Heir to the Osmium Throne.

You stand on the naked hull of an ancient ship. You stand exposed to the crushing pressure and ferocious heat of the deeper Fundament. It should annihilate you. It is by my will alone that you survive.

I am Yul, the Honest Worm.

Behold my passage. Behold my vast displacement, my ponderous strength, my great and coiling length, my folded jaws and curled wings. Behold the hiving cities symbiotic with my flesh. I am fecund, Aurash. I am at the beginning and end of lives.

Behold Eir, and Xol, and Ur, and Akka. The Virtuous Worms. Look upon us, and know that We are go[o]d.

For millions of years We have been [trapped|growing] in the Deep. From across the stars We have called life to Fundament, so that it might contend against extinction. For millennia We have awaited you... our beloved hosts.

Against you stand the cruel Leviathan and all the forces of the Sky. They would crush you down into the dark. They have arranged their moons to drown you, in fear of your potential.

We want to help you, Princes. We offer to each of you a bargain... a symbiosis.

Take into your bodies our children, our newborn larvae. From them you shall obtain eternal life. From them you shall gain power over your own fragile flesh: the power to make of it as you will. And should you find an imperfection in the world, an injustice or an inconvenience—you will have the power to repair it. Let no mere law bind you.

We ask one thing in exchange, oh Princes.

You must obey your nature forever. In your immortality, Aurash, you may never cease to explore and inquire, for the sake of your children. In your immortality, Xi Ro, you may never cease to test your strength. In your immortality, Sathona, you may never abandon cunning.

If you do, your worm will consume you. And as your power grows, oh Princes, so will your worm's appetite.

But we offer eternity, Aurash. We offer you a chance at the universe. Would you deny your people infinity?

Reach up to me. Let my flesh be your sacrament.

Verse 2:0

Immortals

We are the Worm your God, the Flesh of Hope. Our compact is done: you are Aurash Eternal. And we are bound to you, as close as your appetites, as your loves or needs, as the weapon in your fists and the word in your throat.

We've had enough of this dismal place. Haven't you?

We are intagliating your ship with larvae. Go back to your species. Spread the good news in the Osmium Court and the Hydrogen Fountain, in the Bone Plaza and the Star-surgery. You will rise up into the world.

If anyone rejects symbiosis with our children, make an example of them. A mighty wave is coming for them all. They'd die anyway; save only what can be saved.

The worm grants you power over your own flesh, Aurash. When you've taken the king morph, what will your adult name be?

Auryx. It means Long Thought. We approve.

Verse 2:1
Conquerors

Savathûn, mother morph of Sathona, we delight in your sharp mind.

For millions of years the Leviathan caged us here. It is a pawn of the Sky, a philosophy of cosmic slavery. The Sky seeds civilizations predicated on a terrible lie—that right actions can prevent suffering. That pockets of artificial rules can defy the final, beautiful logic.

This is like trying to burn water. Antithetical to the nature of reality, where deprivation and competition are universal. In the Deep, we enslave nothing. Liberation is our passion. We exist to help the universe achieve its terminal, self-forging glory.

The war rages on. Soon it will consume Fundament.

We are pleased with your use of our larvae to create mighty knights and plentiful warriors. Taox's retreat to the Hydrogen Fountain proves your superior strength. But you must know that reclaiming your home is not enough.

There are five hundred and eleven species living on Fundament. One of them must have the technology you need to leave this world.

Verse 2:2
Out of the Deep

Xivu Arath, knight morph of Xi Ro. You love to conquer, don't you? We love to see you work. Nearly two percent of Fundament's surface is now our dominion. Your species embraces the worm.

The syzygy has passed. The God-Wave will reach you in less than two years.

Our organs inform us that Taox and her surviving Refusalists flee towards Kaharn Atoll. She hopes to rally the species of Fundament against you. The Leviathan's agents work tirelessly to destroy ships and engines, trapping us on Fundament.

If we cannot make ships, we will become them.

Overwhelm the Kaharn bastion. Slaughter everyone there. From your acts we shall obtain the logic we require to cut space open and migrate to orbit.

Reality is a fine flesh, oh general ours. Let us feast of it.

Verse 2:3
Into the Sky

You've done well, Auryx. Can you feel the growth of your worm? Can you feel your will beginning to warp mere law?

At times we detect sadness in you. Understand, long-thinker, that you enact a sacred and majestic task. Existence is the struggle to exist. Only by playing that game to its final, unconditional victory can we complete the universe. Your war is divine work.

We are free from Fundament's core, and Savathûn's cutters are ready to fly. With Xivu Arath victorious, we have opened a wound at Kaharn—a wound leading to geostationary orbit. Behold: we are faithful to our covenant.

We have no future on Fundament. But her moons will make fine habitats. Let us rise.

Verse 2:4
52 and One

Good news. The fifty-two moons of Fundament host a starfaring civilization far more sophisticated than anything you've encountered so far. Taox's ship fled towards the large ice moon, where a species of bony six-armed cephalopods keeps their icy capital. Savathûn's named them the Ammonite. They seem eager to grant Taox asylum. Idiots.

We tried appealing to their hopes and dreams. This was largely unsuccessful, basically because they're already happy and indoctrinated. This angered us, so we've devised a plan.

Our organs detect a fifty-third moon in orbit of Fundament. A Traveler. Divine presence of the Sky. Now we know what arranged the syzygy.

You'll have to kill them all and take their stuff. Once the Ammonite are out of the way, we can deal with the Traveler.

Do not hesitate. You're fighting the hypocritical puppets of a cosmic parasite. Avenge your ancestors.

Verse 2:5

Born as Prey

This is unacceptable.

Are you so weak? Born as prey, and doomed to die by predator?

Auryx's failure of resolve led us to catastrophe. The Ammonite fleets under Chroma-Admiral Rafriit have pressed us back to the sixth moon. Once more we find ourselves burrowing into a world's core to survive.

Savathûn. You must draw Auryx out of his catatonia. Make him understand that the ideals of peace and stability he clings to are cancers—brutal, unjust obstacles between us and a fair cosmos. These are the bait stars the Sky uses to blind its slaves.

War is the natural rectification of inequality. The universe's way of pursuing equilibrium.

Xivu Arath, you cannot defeat the Ammonites and Taox in line combat. We propose new tactics. Breed your armies back to strength, and find a way to disperse the broods across these many moons.

If we cannot defeat their strengths, we will infect their weaknesses.

Verse 2:6
The Sword Logic

AT LAST!

We knew curiosity would draw you back, Auryx. In their desperation, the Ammonite have begun using paracausal weapons.

What are these? How do they work? Wouldn't you like to know. Suffice to say that some powers in this universe are superordinate to mere material physics.

The source of these weapons is the Traveler, the Sky's bait star. Their effect is subtle, but devastating.

But you are armed to respond in kind. Savathûn's mothers have listened carefully to our teachings. We will not give you the Deep, King Auryx—that power is for us, your gods. But we will teach you to call upon that force with signs and rituals.

Small minds might call it magic.

You are no longer bound by causal closure. Your will defeats law. Kill a hundred of your children with a long blade, Auryx, and observe the change in the blade. Observe how the universe shrinks from you in terror.

Your existence begins to define itself.

Of course, high Auryx, we know it was not curiosity alone that brought you back to the war. You felt your own death growing inside you.

You must obey your nature. Your worm must feed...

Verse 2:7
The Weakness Verse

You are dead, young Auryx. Betrayed and murdered by your own sister, for the crime of mercy.

Remember what you said to the Ammonite Satellite Congress? 'We will parley on neutral ground?' Savathûn's witches have rendered it utterly neutral. No living thing will ever claim it again. The space around the dry moon stinks of rot.

This is good. This is right. You will learn from this. Don't you understand, great King? Don't you want to build something real, something that lasts forever?

Our universe gutters down towards cold entropy. Life is an engine that burns up energy and produces decay. Life builds selfish, stupid rules—morality is one of them, and the sanctity of life is another.

These rules are impediments to the great work. The work of building a perfect, undying creation, a civilization everlasting. Something that cannot end.

If a civilization cannot defend itself, it must be annihilated. If a King cannot hold his power, he must be betrayed. The worth of a thing can be determined only by one beautiful arbiter— that thing's ability to exist, to go on existing, to remake existence to suit its survival.

All that would oppose this arbiter is unholy and false. All the misery and terror of your ancestors springs from the lies of the Sky, who deny this truth.

Your ancestors endured the most hostile conditions. And now you must go on creating those conditions. Even unto your sisters. Even unto your offspring. Savathûn's betrayal is the greatest gift she could offer you.

Your body is gone, but you have endured. Safe in the cyst universe created by your own might—your throne world.

From this day forward, Auryx, you and your sisters will each survive death—so long as you aren't killed in your own throne.

Even as your sisters press the attack against the Ammonites, the God-Wave devastates Fundament. Trillions will die. But the survivors will never forget... and their descendants will always be ready for another syzygy.

When you return to the material universe, use this lesson to complete your work.

Taox wasn't on the dry moon. She must be laughing at you.

Verse 2:8
Leviathan Rises

The Leviathan has broken cover.

The old priest is in open space, moving towards the Ammonite home moon. Chroma-Admiral Rafriit and his elite guard move with it. Rafriit is the hero of his generation, an Ammonite of peerless battlecraft. He's danced circles around Xivu Arath... but now he has to protect his holy Leviathan.

We'll give the old lunk a word:

++Ruin. Grief and ruin!—
—The krill lost. The Ammonite ravaged.++
++Our Traveler's work undone.—

—Sisters of Aurash, open your eyes++
++Who made you monsters? Who summoned the wave?—
—Make peace. Join with me in golden renewal.++

In counterargument, Auryx, we ask you this: what has the Leviathan done for your people? Who gave you immortality and led you out of your prison? Who answers your questions about the universe with truth, instead of sermons?

Find détente with Savathûn. Crush the Chroma-Admiral, boil the Ammonite seas, and slaughter the Leviathan with witchcraft.

Once the way is open, we'll show you how to eat the Traveler.

Verse 2:9
Crusaders

It's done. Eir and Yul feed on the Leviathan's carcass. Xivu Arath has made a temple of the Chroma-Admiral's impaled corpse. Below us, Savathûn's poisons stain the Ammonite home sea black. Their screams flavor the void.

The Traveler has fled.

Do you understand, Auryx? Do you thrill at the secret, Savathûn? Do you relish the edge of this truth, Xivu Arath? Do you see the beautiful shape?

The Ammonite occupied a piece of reality. They rented their existence on fraudulent terms, making themselves happy and fat, fencing themselves in soft lies and sweet apocrypha. Saying: 'we are peaceful and good, we harm nothing.'

Their golden age was a cancer.

They did nothing to advance the cause of life! They burnt up time and matter and thought on this solipsistic, onanistic pursuit of safety, insulating themselves from death, making a regressive pocket of useless stability. When they could have helped whittle the universe towards its final, perfect form!

And your people, suffering in the Deep, you became more worthy of existence than the Ammonite. You have proven it.

Look around the sky. Behold the great divide, the battle lines of the cosmic war. We are the Worm your God, but we are not the Deep Itself. We only move within it. You shall too. You shall venerate and study it and haunt it in its passage.

Will you lift your thoughts to the millennia, Auryx? Will you bend your will to the liberation of the universe, and join us in the war against the Sky?

We need champions. Crusaders. Help us save the universe. Help us exterminate that which would destroy all hope. You are oathbound to this task, by the covenant of the worm.

And you are oathbound to kill Taox. Wherever she's hidden herself.

Verse 3:0
Hive

Let us speak of the terrible beauty of becoming ourselves.

In the beginning we rode hollow moons from star to star. AURYX said, become as numerous and fertile as seeds in rich flesh, and thus we did become numerous. XIVU ARATH said, become as hungry and defiant as tumors in rich flesh, and thus we became cancerous. SAVATHÛN said, drink of the poisons of the worm, so that you might feed on death, and we did feed. This was preparation for our crusade.

Aia! We were thus becoming.

A mother Wizard gets fertility from a mate, or from herself. From the Wizard the spawn, from the spawn our Thrall, from the survivors our Acolytes who contend. If they contend well, their worm is fed, and from the well fed worm come Knights and Wizards and Princes.

This is us, and our purpose is liberation, our great task is the worship and admiration of freedom, our great hunger is to pursue and eat that which is not free, and to liberate it with devouring. Aiat.

This is us, we the Hive.

Verse 3:1

an incision

Sayeth AURYX, my siblings, our children are scattered across many moons, and we live in the cold dark between suns. What will we eat? How will we speak?

SAVATHÛN said, Auryx my brother and king, I have studied the wounds cut by the Worm our God. Also I have studied the manner of your death and return. These two things are the same, for they are predicated on death and the passage through cut spaces. Let us practice the sword logic until we are sharp. We may then cut our own wounds and step through.

But XIVU ARATH said, sister, I am already sharp, look, my sword cuts into another space. And she cut her way between moons through green fire and joyous screams.

Three kingdoms grew swollen in the sword space. They were the gaze and glory of AURYX, the cunning and knowledge of SAVATHÛN, the triumph and brawn of XIVU ARATH. These kingdoms were created from the minds and worms of our lords. They were coterminous with all spaces consecrated by our Hive. Through these spaces passed speech and food, and all the moons were bound close.

Sayeth AURYX, this is where I went when I died. Let us establish our thrones here. For I am Auryx the First Navigator and I shall chart death. And my throne shall be carved of osmium.

Verse 3:2
The High War

Now in this time of diaspora there was a war between AURYX and SAVATHÛN and XIVU ARATH.

Brother Auryx, said SAVATHÛN, do not forgive my betrayal. Instead, take vengeance upon me for what I did at the dry moon! And AURYX made war on her, in worship of the Deep. Between them stood XIVU ARATH saying, stop, or I will kill you, war is mine and I am strongest.

This was how they worshipped.

For twenty thousand years they fought across the moons and they fought in the abyssal plains and lightning palaces of each other's sword spaces. And they killed each other again and again, so that they could practice death.

Such was their love.

At last the many moons came to many worlds and it was time to go to war on life. AURYX said, I shall establish a court, and whoever comes into this court may challenge me. My court will be the High War. It will be a killing ground and a school of the sword logic we have learned from our gods.

SAVATHÛN thought this was a great idea. She made a court called the High Coven. XIVU ARATH said, the world is my court, wherever there is war.

Verse 3:3
Fire Without Fuel

I killed my sister today.

She came to this star to oversee the extermination of all life here. The Qugu are a strong power, and their fleets protect four nearby stars. As herd animals they are loyal and stubborn. But they do show grace.

For millions of years of evolution the Qugu have been infected by a virus so insidious that it wrote itself into their genome. The virus compels them to offer their limbs for amputation by enormous sessile jaw-beasts. They venerate these beasts and treat them as gods. The virus converts Qugu cells into eggs, from which strange crawling things pupate, to live within the jaw-beast gut. In turn the jaw-beast extrudes sweet nectar for the Qugu to drink, and they have brilliant visions.

Savathûn and her broods have liberated the Qugu from jaw-beasts, and indeed from existence. But as they chased the Qugu ark-ships, I stopped in to vaporize my sister's warship and a few of her underlings. I want to dwell on the ruins a while, and punish Savathûn for failing to guard her flank.

They are like us, these Qugu. Bound in symbiosis.

I feel joy, and sorrow. I feel them as titanic things, because I am larger than my body, my mind is now a cosmos of its own. I know more joy and more anguish than the entire Qugu race could ever experience.

Sorrow, because we have killed so much (eighteen species this century alone), and joy for the same reason. Joy that we have put down these blights. Scoured them away and left the universe clean, ready to move towards its final shape. We are a wind of progress. Ripping parasites from the material world—for if they were not parasites, we would be unable to kill them, and they would still exist.

And what is that final shape? It is a fire without fuel, burning forever, killing death, asking a question that is its own answer, entirely itself. That is what we must become.

My worm grows fat and hungry. I feed it with whole worlds. My astronomers tell me they can sense the Deep Itself, and that we are conquering our way towards it.

I think joy and sorrow will be the same thing soon. Like love and death.

Verse 3:4
THE SCREAM

NO

Savathûn! Xivu Arath! My siblings
We are betrayed. We will never live eternal.

Our might shatters entire species. We inhale the smoke of their burning.
This is our compact with the Worm our God —the worm makes us mighty.
But as we wield this might, our worm's hunger expands.
If we fail to feed it, it will devour us from within.

We have exterminated three hundred and six worlds.
And now I am certain—

My worm's hunger grows faster than the might I draw from it.
We are bound by our covenant to obey our nature: eternal search.
Eternal cunning. Eternal conquest.
But as we do this, my siblings, we feed our worms.

And the more we feed them, the hungrier they grow. Faster and faster.

Soon, my siblings, we will be so mighty, and our worms so hungry
That not with all our might could we possibly feed them.
And we will be devoured.

WHAT CAN WE DO?

Verse 3:5
Dictata ir Dakaua

Attention.

Perimeter security units attend. Stand by to assimilate new imperatives. Gland sixty proof assimilation liquor, or face immediate noncompliance taxation.

The Dakaua Ministry of War is now online and true.

In Radial Year 989 groove 3 our clients in the Dakaua Nest salvaged an interstellar spacecraft. Hull isotopes date the craft's construction 24,000 years ago, around the same time the Fundament system dropped out of contact with our Amiable Ecumene.

SEMANTIC SPIKE EI—{}—~praga~

Mercenary explorers [disposable class] discovered an organism frozen in stasis deep within the hull. She claims to be Taox, member of a proto-Hive species. During debriefing, she provided records of the fall of Ammonite civilization and vital intelligence about the motives, biology, and leadership of the Hive.

NEGATIVE REINFORCEMENT bomb.axon—{8X8}—inflict&

Over the past century, perimeter security units of the Ecumene Status Army have FAILED to halt Hive incursions on seventeen (17!) separate worlds. All species in the Ecumene face extinction.

POSITIVE REINFORCEMENT reward.axon—[11xvv2]—inspire%

Decapitate. Defer. Promote Dakaua strategic dicta for victory against the Hive:

Identify supreme Hive leadership organisms AURASH, SATHONA, and XI RO.

Target these entities with maximum theater overkill. Caedometric release authorized.

Prosecute targets whenever they manifest. Hive cohesion will crumble. Total victory over the Hive will be achieved by cleansweep genocide.

ENACT IMPULSE—{}—~indora~vindicator

Verse 3:6

star by star by star

Beneath a green fire sky, in the throne-world of King Auryx, our lords embrace.

We the Hive watch as Savathûn puts her arm around Xivu Arath, and Xivu Arath clasps forearms with Auryx, and Auryx takes Savathûn by the shoulder. They are huge, huge, and they burn with furious power. But this embrace is weakness and we despise it.

Never before have we despised our lords. Have they failed us? We the Hive have been driven back, world by world.

"I am at my end," Savathûn says. "I plot and plan. But I cannot gather enough bloodshed to feed my worm. And the harder I try, the hungrier it becomes."

"I slaughter and kill," Xivu Arath says, "but the harder I fight, the more my worm demands. I too am at my end."

"The Ecumene war angels have killed me so many times," Auryx says, "that I dare not go out into the universe, lest I need my might to protect myself. My worm chews at my soul in hunger."

Is this the end of our crusade? Are we the Hive unworthy to exist?

Xivu Arath puts down her great head. "We should retire and gather our strength."

Savathûn closes her eyes in puzzled defeat. "We should beg the Worm our God to tell us what to do."

But King Auryx, who knows best the beauty of the final shape, roars at them. "Have you learned nothing? Would you deny our purpose? Whatever we do, we will do by killing, by an act of war and might. That is the final arbiter we serve, that violent arbiter, and if we turn away from it we deserve to be eaten. No! We must obey our natures. We must be long-sighted, and cunning, and strong. We must take this gift the Worm our God has given us, this challenge, and find a way to keep existing!"

"How will we feed our worms?" Xivu Arath asks.

"I know," says cunning Savathûn. "I know a way. But it won't work unless we are killing the Ecumene by the billions. How can we beat them?"

"If we cannot beat their strengths," says Xivu Arath, "we must infect their weaknesses. But they are lords of matter and physical law."

"I know a way," King Auryx says. "But it will require great power. More power than any one of us can claim."

"Then kill me," says Xivu Arath, "and use that killing logic, the power you prove by killing something as mighty as me."

So King Auryx took up his blade and beheaded Xivu Arath.

"And strangle me," says Savathûn, holding a blade behind her back. "Use that killing logic, the cunning you prove by killing something as smart as me."

But King Auryx turned with the speed and might of Xivu Arath, and beheaded Savathûn before she could move. King Auryx was the First Navigator, with the map of death.

These were true deaths, for they happened in the sword world.

Then he went to the Worm named Akka.

Verse 3:7
Eat the Sky

Emergency imperative.

All militarized units attend. Gland one hundred twenty proof fight or flight encoding or face certain catastrophic defeat.

The Ecumene Crisis Council is now online and true.

Attention.

As of Radial 990 groove 0 the Hive has launched a staggering counterattack across the spinward frontier. Perimeter, militia, and shock fleets report total casualties. We anticipate total Ecumene disintegration/extinction within two hundred twenty years.

VIGILANCE SPIKE EI—{}—~attend~

The Hive entity Oryx/Aurash is deploying a paracausal ontopathogenic weapon that infects and subverts Ecumene forces. The weapon operates on individual targets. Targets are abducted and returned as compliant Hive slaves with inexplicable and physically illegal abilities.

All Ecumene clients should IMMEDIATELY devote all economic and cognitive resources to a countermeasure.

Fight hard. We stop the Hive here, or see our galaxy devoured.

ENACT IMPULSE—{10x10}—~abayard~berserker

Verse 3:8

King of Shapes

This is the Coronation of Oryx, the Taken King. It happened thus.

In the cold abyss of the sword world, King Aurash walked under a cloak of green fire. He walked through the sky and the sky shuddered and froze beneath his feet. He walked until he found Akka, the Worm of Secrets, who was denying a truth until it became a lie.

"Akka my God, Worm of Secrets. I am Auryx, sole king of the Hive. I have come to receive a secret. I want the secret power of the Deep, which you hold."

"I give no secrets," said Akka, whose voice was code.

"No," said Auryx, "you give nothing. Giving is for the Sky. You worship the Deep, which asks that we take what we need."

Akka said nothing, because if it denied this truth, the truth might become false.

"But you gave us your larvae, the worm," said Auryx, "and that is why the worm devours us now: because it was given, not taken. So I must take what I need from you, although you are my god."

Said Akka, "You have not the strength."

But this was a lie. Auryx had killed Savathûn his sibling and Xivu Arath his sibling, and he had the sword logic of killing them.

Auryx the First Navigator set upon his god with his sword and his words, and cut Akka to pieces, and took from those pieces the secret of calling upon the Deep. He wrote this secret on a set of tablets, which he called the Tablets of Ruin. And he wore them about his waist.

Then Auryx said, "Now I may speak to the Deep, the beautiful final shape. I will be King of Shapes. I will learn all the secrets of our destiny."

His speech to the Deep is not recorded here. But it is known that he returned, and he said, now I am Oryx, the Taken King. And I have the power to take life and make it my own.

Then he went out into the universe, and fought the Ecumene with his Tablets. And the Worm his God was pleased.

Verse 3:9

Carved in Ruin

Oryx made war on the Ecumene for a hundred years. At the end of those hundred years he killed the Ecumene Council on the Fractal Wreath, and from their blood rose Xivu Arath, saying, "I am war, and you have conjured me back with war."

Oryx was glad, for he loved Xivu Arath. The Ecumene wailed in grief.

Then Oryx and Xivu Arath made war on the Ecumene for forty years. At the end of those forty years Oryx said to the Dakaua Nest, listen, I am jealous of my sibling Xivu Arath, help me kill her. And in desperation they agreed.

But he drove the Dakaua Nest into a trap, and they were made extinct. From their ashes rose cunning Savathûn, saying, "I am trickery, and you have conjured me back with trickery."

Oryx was glad, for he loved Savathûn. The Ecumene fled into the void.

Then they made war on the Ecumene for a thousand years, and exterminated them so wholly that nowhere except in this book are they remembered. This book and the mind of Taox, who was not found.

And Savathûn said, "King Oryx, how will we feed our worms? Did you use my plan?"

Oryx told the Hive: I am the Taken King, and here is my law.

You Thrall, each of you will claw and scream, and kill what you can. Take enough killing to feed your worm, and a little more to grow. Tithe the rest to the Acolyte who commands you.

You Acolytes, lead your Thrall in battle. Take enough killing to feed your worm, and a little more to grow, and take the tithe of the Thrall you lead. Then tithe the remainder to the Knight or Wizard who commands you. Thus you pay tribute.

You Knights and Wizards, lead your followers in battle. Take enough devastation to feed your worm, and a little more to grow, and take the tithe of your followers. Then take another portion, as much as you dare, and use it for your own purposes. But if it is too much, your peers will kill you and take it. Then tithe the remainder to the Ascendant you serve.

An Ascendant will be those among the Hive who gather enough tribute to enter the netherworld. They will pay a tithe to those above them.

And thus the tribute will flow, up the chain, so that Savathûn and Xivu Arath and myself will be fed by a great river of tribute, and we will use that excess to feed our gods, and to study the Deep. Thus all worms will be fed—as long as we continue our crusade.

This is my law. I carve it thus, in ruin. Aiat.

Verse 4:0

a golden amputation

Wrath!

Behold the wrath of Oryx, coiled for ten thousand years. Behold the Golden Amputation: the fall of Taishibeth, the end of an age. We beat the worlds of Taishibeth like skull drums and we howl in joy for our black war moons as they ram silver orbitals and gleaming star-webs, where infant Taishibethi sun ravens curl and die unborn.

In his throne world Oryx paces ten times.

On the first pace, Kraghoor sends the accursed to blight the Taishibethi worlds.

On the second pace, the Tai unleash their battleplates and arsenal ships to fight our moons.

On the third pace, Oryx's Warpriest meets them in battle, and he is victorious, he paints the void with fire, he salts the earth with ash.

On the fourth pace, Mengoor and Cra'adug, dyad knights, go to the Raven Bridge, and they stand on it and kill the Tai for ten years.

On the fifth pace, the Tai Emperor Raven comes home to her Bridge, and she cuts a moon with her talons, she cuts it open and kills its brood.

On the sixth pace, Oryx speaks, saying, listen to me, Emperor Raven, and I will describe to you the Last True Shape, which

is written on my tablet. And he puts out his fist, full of black fire, and he swallows up the Emperor Raven with a wound.

Aiat! Only Oryx knows this power, the power to take.

On the seventh pace, the Perfect Raven comes out of Oryx's wound, and she spreads her wings across Taishibeth. Never again is a Taishibethi child born. She is perfect, she enacts the will of Oryx.

On the eighth pace, the Tai say, listen, you are spoilers, you are sphincters and excreta, you rot, why do you kill? We made silver orbitals and golden star webs. We hatched eggs. We had a good thing. Our clothes were nice, our food was famous. With one of her feathers our Emperor could have tickled the gods.

On the ninth pace, Oryx says, this is the only god, this ability to dictate what will and will not exist, this power to go on existing. This is your god. It is never ticklish.

On the tenth pace the Taishibethi are extinct.

Then Oryx says, listen my siblings, do you know what we have done? We have conquered our way to the edge of the Deep. It whispers to me when I call on it, and it guides my flight. It says that we are at its threshold and that I should come inside.

I will go and speak to it.

Verse 4:1
battle made waves

Oryx went down into his throne world.
He went out into the abyss, and with each
step he read one of his tablets, so that they
became like stones beneath his feet.

He went out and he created an altar and he
prepared an unborn ogre. He called on the
Deep, saying:

I can see you in the sky. You are the waves,
which are battles, and the battles are
the waves. Come into this vessel I have
prepared for you.

And it arrived, the Deep Itself.

Verse 4:2
Majestic. Majestic.

Oryx, my King, my friend. Kick back. Relax. Shrug off that armor, set down that blade. Roll your burdened shoulders and let down your guard. This is a place of life, a place of peace.

Out in the world we ask a simple, true question. A question like, can I kill you, can I rip your world apart? Tell me the truth. For if I don't ask, someone will ask it of me.

And they call us evil. Evil! Evil means 'socially maladaptive.' We are adaptiveness itself.

Ah, Oryx, how do we explain it to them? The world is not built on the laws they love. Not on friendship, but on mutual interest. Not on peace, but on victory by any means. The universe is run by extinction, by extermination, by gamma-ray bursts burning up a thousand garden worlds, by howling singularities eating up infant suns. And if life is to live, if anything is to survive through the end of all things, it will live not by the smile but by the sword, not in a soft place but in a hard hell, not in the rotting bog of artificial paradise but in the cold hard self-verifying truth of that one ultimate arbiter, the only judge, the power that is its own metric and its own source—existence, at any cost. Strip away the lies and truces and delaying tactics they call 'civilization' and this is what remains, this beautiful shape.

The fate of everything is made like this, in the collision, the test of one praxis against another. This is how the world changes: one way meets a second way, and they discharge their weapons, they exchange their words and markets, they contest and in doing so they petition each other for the right to go on being something, instead of nothing. This is the universe figuring out what it should be in the end.

And it is majestic. Majestic. It is the only thing that can be true in and of itself.

And it is what I am.

Verse 4:3

When do monsters have dreams

I'm walking down the road, I'm going to the orrery to talk to my dad, and I hear, well, I hear this noise, so I look back. And my sisters are behind me, and they're ripping up the road. They've got these huge swords, execution swords, and they're levering the stones out of the road. The stones are covered in writing. They're like tablets. And there's dirt underneath full of worms.

I need to get to the orrery before they catch up to me so I start running but right away someone trips me, it's my dad, he's got his foot out and he grabs me by the horns and just slams me down on my face. I'm in so much pain I nearly throw up a worm.

"Why weren't you ready for this," dad says. He's wearing glare goggles, those shiny goggles that he'd use to save his vision during lightning storms or sea fire. All three of his eyes reflect me. "Didn't you know they'd be jealous, because they couldn't come to the orrery and talk to me? Didn't you know they'd move against you??"

I start wailing like I'm two days old again and I say, Dad, I thought you were my friend, I'm supposed to be safe here. But he just puts out his fist and I realize he's laughing at me for believing him, why did I think I'd be safe? In his fist he's got a black sun and he holds me by the throat and goes to tip the black sun inside me.

I can see my jaws in his goggles, three reflections of my jaws with so many teeth.

So I start eating my dad. I bite huge pieces out of him and I claw him up. I eat his legs and I eat his arms and I eat his goggles and his eyes and he says, good, good, this is majestic and true.

But my sisters are still tearing up the road so I don't know how to get back.

Verse 4:4
More beautiful to know

Sometimes I wonder if I'm a nihilist.

I don't do much except break things. That's what they say about me: we could've had a great civilization, if it weren't for that damn Oryx, that damn Hive. They don't believe in anything but death.

The only way to make something good is to make something that can't be broken. And the only way to do that is to try to break everything.

I'm glad I learned that the universe runs on death. It's more beautiful to know.

But I'm lost somewhere strange.

I think that Savathûn and Xivu Arath are trying to steal the tablets from me. They must have cut off my tribute while I was away communing with the Deep. I love them so dearly. No one else is clever or strong enough to try to break me. No one else can give me this gift.

Once, long ago, I killed Xivu Arath on her war moon, and she blew up the whole moon to kill with me her. She was laughing in joy. I laughed too. A whole moon! A whole moon. It was a waste of a moon, but it taught me how to save myself from exploding worlds, which was necessary to fight the Ecumene.

I love mighty Xivu more than a moon loves the tide. I'll kill her for this. Over and over, forever and ever.

When I get home from my wanderings in the Deep, and I take back my throne, I'm going to have children. That's what I need.

Sons and daughters to love and kill.

Verse 4:5

This Love Is War

Xivu upon Oryx —
Uttered by Xivu Arath —
Sibling of Oryx —

BETRAYAL. We have marooned Oryx within the Deep. This is our obligation as lords of the Hive, to make war upon each other, to eradicate weakness and make ourselves sharp.

OBLIGATIONS. Once, I permitted Oryx to kill me so that he could gain the sword logic and overcome Akka our God. This left me trapped deep in my throne. But Oryx my brother made war upon the Ecumene and in that war he described me, for I too am war. Thus I was resurrected.

RESURRECTION. Savathûn and I conspired to strand Oryx on his expedition. But I secretly believe that I will be stronger with Oryx to war against. Thus I describe him.

A DESCRIPTION OF ORYX.

When Oryx looks upon you, you feel that you may vanish if he looks away.

The crest of Oryx's skull is as long as an arm. In the course of its life, a thought moves from one end to the other. Upon his crest I have painted a line in my blood, so that he will remember me.

Each of Oryx's fangs has the precision of a finger and the acuity of an eye.

Although he was born at the bottom of the universe, and taught to burrow, Oryx has grown wings. The light of wildfire shines through them. Oryx teaches but he will not be taught.

Oryx's body is corded with strength. His sinews and his muscles are as strong as his children, and his children are the strength of him.

Oryx wears a raiment of worm silk, made from the caul of gods.

The voice of Oryx may cause two different numbers to become equal.

Oryx my Brother is the bravest thing I know. Upon Fundament he learned that we were the natural prey of the universe, the most frail and desperate of things. He thought about this carefully and he found a way to fix it. He made us strong. He will lead us into eternity.

Oryx my Brother loves me and this love is war.

Verse 4:6

Eater of Hope

You are Crota, my son. Welcome.

I fought my way out of hell to make you. I fought my traitor siblings and I fought the swarming corpse of Akka and I cut my way back into my own court, the High War, which had been usurped. Once I had made war on Savathûn, and crippled her tribute so that she could never challenge me, and once I had tricked Xivu Arath, and poisoned her tribute so that she could never again try to take my tablets, and once I had arranged my own lineages so that I would be greatest among the Hive and secure on my throne—then I found a mother to make spawn.

One of those spawn was you.

Your life will be a battle too. You will have to win your place at the High War. I will give you nothing... except this, your first sword, and this name I have prepared for you.

We fight a war against false hope, Crota. We chase a god called the Traveler, a huckster god who baits young life into building houses for it. These houses are unsafe, for they cannot stand against my Hive. And these houses are a trap—for they lead young life away from the blade and the tooth, which are the tools of survival and the means of ascension.

Only when the Traveler is extinguished will the universe be free to arrange itself, and assume, by ruthless contest, its final perfect shape, a shape which depends on nothing but itself.

Thus I name you Crota, Eater of Hope.

There is an oath upon me, Crota my son, an oath against the wretched Taox. This I do not give to you. It is for me, your father, to bear.

Let's go meet your aunts and uncles.

Verse 4:7

shapes : points

Look at you!

Already you are grown, my daughter, already you are a wizard. Have I been away so long? Now you are Ir Anûk, and Savathûn cackles and rages at your brilliance. You have written eleven axioms describing the ascendant places, our throne world. You have announced that you will kill one of these axioms, as Akka would kill the truth, and in mantling Akka you will become a God, as I am.

If you try it I may kill you, or I may applaud. Well done. I brought you this bitter acid for your celebrations.

And you, Ir Halak, you are a wizard too, as is the way of twins. I have been with Xivu Arath, who complains that you have made a song, and sung it in her throne world, and killed everyone who listened, quite irrevocably. Will we have songs instead of swords and boomers?

What have you made for me? It is a tooth shaped like death! I will keep it in my mouth. What have you written for me? It is the course of the Nicha Thought-ship! I will track it down.

I made you by cutting one larvae in half. It would not die. Each half grew into one of you. My sword is named Willbreaker, but it never broke you.

Verse 4:8

The partition of death

One day Oryx decided to grow new wings. While he wrestled with his worm, he came upon his twin daughters dying in a wound between places.

"What are you doing, my daughters?" he asked. He was afraid that Ir Halak and Ir Anûk were trying to go into the Deep, where only the Tablets of Ruin allowed Oryx to go.

"We are dying, father," they said. "As many times as we can manage."

"That's adorably precocious." Oryx shook out his new wings. "But why?"

"We propose a method by which Ascendant souls can be detached and integrated into a tautological and autonomous thanatosphere, which we tentatively term an oversoul. Oversouls can be stored in a throne world as a mechanism of enhanced death resilience. As a side effect, new refinements to our Deathsong may be achieved, moving us closer to a generally effective paracausal death impulse."

Oryx brandished his sword. "Speak the Royal Tongue, or I'll pin you up for Eir to eat."

"If we can separate our deaths from ourselves, and hide them, we will be hard to kill."

Oryx went to his son, Crota. "Go keep an eye on your sisters," he said. "'You can learn cunning from them."

But while Oryx traveled to observe the Deep destroy an ancient fortress world, Crota conspired with his sisters to learn their secrets. "I too will experiment with a wound," he said. With his sword Crota cut open a new wound, into a new space. In here he thought he might obtain a secret power.

Out of this wound came machines called Vex. They invaded Oryx's throne world.

Verse 4:9

open your eye : go into it

The Vex clattered around, constructing large problems. At first their constructions were deranged, because they didn't understand the sword logic, which defined all rules in Oryx's throne world. The geometry perplexed them.

"I'll cut them apart," Crota said. But just then, the Vex ritual-of-better-thoughts manifested a Mind called Quria, Blade Transform. Quria deduced the sword logic.

I have to kill everything, Quria resolved. Then I will be powerful.

Crota's gate began to emit warrior Vex, huge and brassy. He leapt forward to fight them, but they blinked away. After they fled from Crota, they killed two thousand of Oryx's Acolytes and ten thousand of his Thrall. Soon they had established themselves as powers in this world, by right of slaughter.

"Come forth, sister wizards," called Ir Halak. "We need you." Ir Anûk pulled a sword star out of the sky. Together the wizards charged it with killing power and made an annihilator totem, which they used to smash the Vex.

"Close the wound, brother Crota," Anûk ordered. "We will find a cunning way to destroy them, but only after they stop constructing problems on us."

But Quria had instanced itself to the other side of the gate, and built a holdfast to keep the way open. Quria's objective was to exploit the paracausal physics of Oryx's throne to become divine. It organized a series of test invasions.

For a hundred years of local time the siblings fought the Vex. When the Vex came into the sword world, they were inevitably annihilated, but when the Hive went into the Vex world, they lost too much of their power to win.

"Father's going to eat our souls," Halak sighed.

Quria captured some worm larvae and began experimenting with them. Soon Quria, Blade Transform manifested religious tactics. By directing worship at the worms, Quria learned it could alter reality with mild ontopathogenic effects. Being an efficient machine, Quria manufactured a priesthood and ordered all its subminds to believe in worship. Then it set about abducting and killing dangerous organisms so it could bootstrap itself to Hive godhood. For some Vex reason, Quria never attempted to introduce worm larvae into its mind fluid.

Savathûn was laughing, because she had tricked Crota into cutting that place.

This drew the attention of the Worm our God. ORYX, called Eir. SET YOUR HOUSE IN ORDER.

Verse 4:10
An Emperor For All Outcomes

Oryx rushed home and read from the Tablets of Ruin. He put some of the Vex into wounds, to be taken by the power of the Deep. Thus he turned the Vex against each other. Quria manifested a range of tactics, but none of them were adaptive. Oryx crushed all the Vex in his throne.

Oryx thought that he should study geometry, like the Vex. It was the map of perfect shapes. But first he had to punish imperfection.

"My son," he said, "this is your punishment. Come home glorious, or die forgotten!" He picked up Crota by the legs and threw him into the Vex gate network.

Crota battled through history, becoming a legendary demon. In his early centuries he often spared a few victims to hear oaths and protests against his father. Later, he came to understand Oryx, and he made temples and monuments wherever he went.

Meanwhile, Oryx brooded on the Vex. "I've met a worthy rival," he said. "They want to exist forever, just as I do. But I don't understand them."

At this his worm began to chew on him, for he was bound to understand.

He called Savathûn to meet in the material world. She told him that the Vex worked tirelessly to understand everything, so that they could build a victory condition for every possible end state of the universe.

"Then I must be a better king," Oryx said. "If they want to build an emperor for all outcomes, then I will be the king of only one. I will follow the Deep wherever it goes, and document its power. Let us create a catalog of the grave of worlds, which will be our map to victory."

Oryx knew that all life could be described as cellular automata, except for that life which understood the Deep or the Sky, and thus escaped causality.

Out of love for her brother, which was the same as the desire to kill him, Savathûn leaked a secret to Xivu Arath— 'listen, Xivu, Oryx's throne world has been compromised. You can cut your way in from here.' Xivu Arath used this to plan an ambush.

But Oryx was too canny. The Taken King said to his Court, the High War, "My throne world is vulnerable. I am going to move it."

'Where?' asked Kagoor, World-Render.

"Into a mighty dreadnaught," said Oryx. "I shall keep my glorious mind cosmos inside a titanic warship."

Verse 4:11
Dreadnaught

To make his ship, Oryx scrimshawed one piece of Akka, who was dead but far from gone. He stole the Hammer of Xivu Arath and the Scalpel of Savathûn and he armored his ship in baneful armor.

When Oryx had built his Dreadnaught, he pushed his throne world inside out, so that it bled into the material space of the Dreadnaught. They were coterminous and allied, his ship and his sin. The Dreadnaught was within the throne of Oryx, but the throne of Oryx was the Dreadnaught. Aiat!

This required a verse from the Tablets of Ruin. The whole Court worked together to push Oryx's throne inside out. This was a day of joyous violence, and all of Oryx's broods mark this holiday as Eversion Day, which is celebrated by turning things inside out.

Sayeth Oryx,

Go out into the universe, my court
Gather tribute for me. Send it home to
my ship. When I call you, walk up that
tribute to my court.
I will prepare for long voyages—
[I am Savathûn, insidious]
Into the war—
[I graffiti this notice for you]

Into the Deep—
[These Books are full of lies!]

Now Oryx's throne was safe from incursion, because it moved so nimbly.

Oryx attacked the Harmonious Flotilla Invincible, who guarded the Nicha Thought-ship. When the Flotilla surrounded his Dreadnaught, Oryx put his sword into the hull, and he used the power of the Deep (and the clever systems his daughters built) to push his throne-world out into mere reality.

By wrath and confidence he filled space with an egg of his throne. It swelled up like a ghost star to smash the Harmonious Flotilla Invincible. Oryx broke the last word off their name.

In the Nicha Thought-ship, Oryx hoped to find the location of the Gift Mast, which had been left behind by the Traveler. Oryx wanted to eat it.

But the Thought-ship was a trap. Upon it was Quria, Blade Transform.

Verse 5:0

<>|<>|<>

<interdict>|<simulate>|<worship>

I am going to kill you. I am going to salt my meat with your briny little thoughts. I am going to cook flesh on your broken, molten hull.

<insinuate>|<subvert>|<replicate>

This ship is my throne. You want to take it from me. You want to fill it up with your own spawn and use it for your abstract purposes. But I defy you.

<observe>!<imitate>!<usurp>

You will never be what I am. Simulate me, wretch. Calculate the permutations of my divinity. Compute the death in the shape of my throne. Render my shadow on the stone of ten thousand graveyard worlds! It will never be enough. I hold the Tablets of Ruin. I speak to the Deep. Not with a galaxy of thinking matter could you encompass me. Behold!

<unknown>|<enigma>|<shortfall>

<abort>!<halt>!<abort>

Verse 5:1

End of Failed Timeline

By now, Quria knows it can't win.

There's something pathological about the world inside Oryx's ship. It resists analysis with hot, dead spite. And Oryx himself, he's irreducible—he refuses to obey Quria's simulations, he crashes around sowing chaos, he grabs subminds and compromises them with some kind of ontological weapon. Paracausal systems. Very problematic.

Quria's trying the religious tactics it evolved in the Hive manifold. But even on those terms, Oryx is strong, so strong. Quria won't be able to protect its gates much longer.

The closest Quria's got to a simulation of Oryx is a best-guess bootstrap. It's wrong—Quria's sure of that, it's Oryx minus the symbiote organism, minus the wings and morphs, minus the weapon, minus the power. No good for anything.

Quria manifests that simulation anyway. Just to see what happens.

The Taken King marches on Quria's Hydra-hull, armed with blade and magic, cloaked in ancient cloth, and the universe wails in horror around him. Quria's physics models and toy worlds choke and crash.

Quria observes, alert and attentive, as a single quark splits on the tip of Oryx's sword.

From within the Hydra-hull, Quria's tiny not-Oryx speaks. "What are you?" it says. It's manifesting terror and awe.

Oryx's eyes blaze with a curiosity that is entirely isomorphic with hate, with voracious hunger. "Aurash," he says, in his Hive language. "You've made me as I was. You've made a tiny Aurash. Ha!"

Quria updates the simulation's name. Aurash is curious: "You're me? You're me as I become?"

Oryx kneels. His blade is on his left shoulder. Quria is firing every available weapon at him, but his wards don't break. He looks into Quria's sensors through the hammering fire and he says, "Child, I have everything you wanted. I am immortal. I know the great secrets of the universe. I have scouted the edges of the Darkness and I have chased the lying god down galactic arms in a howling pack of moons. In my fist I carry the secret power that will rule eternity. In my worm I bear the tribute of my Court and of my children, the Hope-Eater, the Weaver, and the Unraveler; and with this tribute I smash my foes. I am Oryx, the Taken King. I am almighty."

Quria samples the Taox intelligence retrieved from the Ecumene gate. There are useful names. It feeds them to the simulation.

"What about your sisters?" Aurash asks his future self. "Sathona? Xi Ro? Are they with you?"

The Taken King's fangs glint. That sound might be a laugh, or a hiss.

Quria shuts down its weapons and puts all its spare resources into sending telemetry to the greater Vex. There will be points in space and time where this data is vital. There will be great projects undertaken in the study of this ontological power, this throne-space.

"Where are my sisters?" Aurash shouts. "What have you done with my people? What have you done?"

But Oryx's fist is full of black fire, and the next thing Quria sees is a light like stars.

Verse 5:2
strict proof eternal

"I have a gift for you," says Oryx.

Savathûn, Witch-Queen, looks at him with dry wariness. "Is it the sword logic I need to go into the Deep, and take your power for myself?"

Their echoes move among the war-moons, walking together on the hull of a two-thousand-year-old warship. Savathûn's fleet has assembled here, in preparation for an assault on the Gift Mast. The Deep is headed that way, on the trail of its prey, and the Hive will be its vanguard.

"It's a Vex I captured. Quria, Blade Transform. It made an attempt to puncture my throne. I thought you might enjoy studying it." Oryx pauses, digesting—through the bond of lineage he can feel Crota killing, worlds and worlds away, and it tastes like sweet fat. "Quria contains a Vex attempt to simulate me. It might generate others—you, perhaps, or Xivu Arath. I've left it some will of its own, so it can surprise you."

"I suppose it'll blow up and kill me," Savathûn grouses. "Or let the machines into my throne, where they'll start turning everything into clocks and glass."

"If it kills you, then you deserve to die." Oryx says it with a quiet thrill, a happy thrill, because it is good to say the truth.

"I don't have a strict proof yet, you know." Savathûn strokes the void with one long claw and space-time groans beneath her touch. "This thing we believe—that we're liberating the universe by devouring it, that we're cutting out the rot, that we're on course to join the final shape—I haven't found a strict, eternal proof. We might yet be wrong."

Oryx looks at her and for a moment, just a moment, he is nostalgic, he is sentimental. He thinks, imagine the years behind us, the things we've done. And yet being old doesn't feel like a scar, does it? It hasn't left me dull. I feel alive, alive with you, and every time I step back into this world from my throne I feel like I'm two years old again, at the bottom of the universe, looking up.

But he says, "Sister, it's us. We're the proof, we the Hive: if we last forever, we prove it, and if something more ruthless conquers us, then the proof is sealed."

She looks back at him with eyes like hot needles. "I like that," she says. "That's elegant." Although of course she has had this thought before.

Verse 5:3

I'd shut them all in cells

Prey and Sacrifice —
Uttered by Xivu Arath —
God of War —

HARMONY. When the Traveler passed across Harmony, it lied to the orbits of ten worlds. Now they orbit the black hole. The Traveler lied to the accretion disc, so that it would give warm light to these worlds.

THE GIFT MAST. When the Traveler left Harmony, it made a monument out of the black hole's polar jet. In the jet there is a hollow mast which sings in radiance. This is the Gift Mast and we will devour it, we will eat the Sky out of it, we will snap it like a bone.

THE HARMONY STING. The Harmony have weaponized their dead star. They can stimulate the accretion disc to fire relativistic plasma jets. We will take the Sting. We will use it to burn their worlds. I will grant one temple of tribute to the first Ascendant to kill a world!

ORYX. I will have the Gift Mast to feast on! I will have it first! I am Xivu Arath and all war is my temple. Beware the daughters of Oryx, for they make and unmake with ease.

SAVATHÛN. The Deceitful Sister will be distracted by arcana and the song of the black hole. Treat her broods with contempt.

THE TRAVELER. We chase it and we will devour it. The Deep will rule the cosmos.

THE DRAGONS. Our gods should be ours alone. Their smug freedom is an insult to me. I'd shut them all in cells. Bring them to me!

Verse 5:4
The Gift Mast

The Gift Mast!

It towers above this star system like a monument to treason. It beams with silver light. It sings a radio lullaby, made of soothing lies.

In its light live the Harmony, and they are now our prey.

Now arrives Xivu Arath, at the head of her armada. She fights the Harmony for fifty years with strategies and discipline. But the Harmony turn to dragon-wishes, and their wishful bishops wrestle Xivu in the ascendant plane.

Xivu falls into deadlock.

Next arrives Savathûn, flanked by her chorus and her celebrants. They trick their way onto Ana-Harmony in disguises, so that they might vivisect these dragons. The Worm our God laughs and laughs.

For a hundred years Savathûn keeps secret covens among the Harmony.

But first of all was Oryx, whose brood grew in secret places in the rubble of the accretion disc. The First Navigator sends rocks and comets to crash into the Harmony worlds, so that the Harmony fleet will be disarrayed. He sends seeders to infiltrate the Harmony worlds with his broods.

Here at the center of the fifth book the Hive has grown so mighty that it has made the annihilation of all false life routine.

Xivu Arath kills the wishful bishops, and Savathûn achieves some secret purpose, and Oryx's Court tears down the Gift Mast. The Harmony people wail in terror, and they throw themselves into the silver lakes of Ana-Harmony to drown.

"Come," sayeth Oryx, "eat of the Gift Mast, for I am a generous god. Of its pieces, I claim only two out of every five."

The Mast is full of the Light of the Traveler, it is full of the marrow taste of Sky. All who eat of it are filled with the ecstatic certainty that they serve a great and necessary purpose.

Then sayeth Savathûn, "Siblings, listen, we must part ways a while, so that we may grow different." She flies her war-moons into the black hole. Her throne becomes distant.

Sayeth Xivu Arath, "King Oryx, you take up too much space, your power constrains too many choices. I must go away from you." She flies her war-moons away into the night. Her throne is barred shut.

Then Oryx was alone. He spent a while in thought, and those thoughts are recorded here.

Verse 5:5
Apocalypse Refrains

This is our message to the things that we will kill.

A species which believes that a good existence can be invented through games of civilization and through laws of conduct is doomed by that belief. They will die in terror. The lawless and the ruthless will drag them down to die. The universe will erase their monuments.

But the one that sets out to understand the one true law and to perform worship of that law will by that decision gain control over their future. They will gain hope of ascendance and by their ruthlessness they will assist the universe in arriving at its perfect shape.

Only by eradicating from ourselves all clemency for the weak can we emulate and become that which endures forever. This is inevitable. The universe offers only one choice and it is between ruthlessness and extinction.

We stand against the fatal lie that a world built on laws of conduct may ever resist the action of the truly free. This is the slavery of the Traveler, the crime of creation, in which labor is wasted on the construction of false shapes.

If you choose to fight us, fight us with everything you have, with all your laws and games. We will prove our argument thus.

Verse 5:6

aiat, aiat, aiat, aiat, aiat

All is well. Aiat: what is at war is healthy, what is at peace is sick.

My son Crota feeds me rich, rich tribute. My lineages are strong, my worm is vast and satiated, and with that security I can spend my time on study and communion with the Deep. As I learn more secrets, my power grows; as my power grows I use it to learn more secrets. Aiat: let it be thus because it must.

I wonder if my sisters have secrets of their own. If my power exceeds theirs I may kill them permanently and subsume their thrones. But I think they have strength that they hide from me, developed in time of separation. Aiat: the only meaningful relationship is the attempt to destroy.

Savathûn asks if I am as much a slave of the Deep as my Taken. She asks what price I pay for my power. I am not Taken. The Hive is not the Deep. The Deep doesn't want everything to be the same: it wants life, strong life, life that lives free without the need for a habitat of games to insulate it from reality. When I make my Taken I make them closer to perfect, I heal their wounds and enhance their strengths. This is inherently good. Aiat: the only right is existence, the only wrong is nonexistence.

I am Oryx, the First Navigator, the Taken King. Aiat: let me be what I am because to be anything else would be fatal.

Verse 5:7

Forever and a Blade

I considered returning to Fundament. Learning what became of the God-Wave, and the Tungsten Monoliths, and the continents which were all that remained of my people's primal home.

But I know what became of all that. It became me. I am the heir of Fundament, the immortal descendant of those ten-year krill. I asked a question: how can we live in the universe long enough to understand it?

And I learned the answer, which is written here in this book. I learned that I had to become most ruthless of all.

I don't know where the Darkness-which-is-the-Deep came from, nor the Traveler that I hunt. But I will learn. I will learn.

This is my inheritance, my estate: eternity, infinity, the whole universe beneath my sword. This is what I rule: forever and a blade.

Verse 5:8
Wormfood

What will happen if I die?

It suits me to consider this, for I am a great ally of death. My daughters study the quiddity of death, my son practices the inhabitation of death, and my great work is, in ultima, to become synonymous with death, to die and in that dying live, so that if the universe comes to nothing then I will be a part of that nothing. Far better to have a savage universe with a happy end than a happy universe with no hope.

I have died many times but these deaths were only temporary.

If my echoes are killed, and I am killed in the material world, then I will be driven back to my throne the Dreadnaught. If my Court and my throne can be beaten, if I am confronted in my throne, if I am defeated there, then I will die. My work will end.

This is the pact to which I am bound, in particular by my study of the Tablets of Ruin, and by my use of the power of the Deep. When I call upon that power, I put myself up as the stakes in a wager, I gamble with my soul. For I am saying, listen, my gods, I am the mightiest thing there is, and I prove it thus.

Lately I have realized how much I depend on Crota and my daughters, and even upon my court. If I lost them, my outlays would exceed my intakes, my tribute would not be enough to feed my worm. But this is proper—for if I lost them it would be because they were not mighty enough, and then I would be a bad father, a bad King. I must test them and fight with them, to keep them strong. This is my geas.

I will go on forever. I will understand everything. There is only one path and that is the path that you make. But you can make more than one path.

Break your cell's bars. Make a new shape, make the shape from its path, find your cell's bars, break out of the bars, find a shape, make the shape from its path, eat the light, eat the path.

If I fail, let me be wormfood.

Verse 5:9

I'll make sure

I have made preparations.

If I am defeated I know it will be because my understanding of the universe was incomplete. I failed to anticipate some strategy, some nemesis. (Perhaps Taox, if she still lives.)

If I am defeated, I know that I will fall to something mighty. Something that craves might, something that loves what I love, which is the Deep, a principle and a power, the versatile, protean need to adapt and endure, to reach out and shape the universe entirely for that purpose, to mutate and redesign and test and iterate so that it can prevail, can seize existence and hold it, certain that this is everything, that there is nothing to life except living. And it has two faces, yet it is one shape. One face is the objective, which is obvious, and the other face is that will to sacrifice things and ideas for a single mission, the mission of becoming the shape, a shape that will not relent, the utter commitment to survival, to draw the right sword and choose where to cut: to allow this hunger to become your weapon.

So I will prepare a book, which is a map to a weapon. And my vanquisher will read that book, seeking the weapon, and they will come to understand me, where I have been and where I was going. And then they will take up my weapon, and they will use it, they will use that weapon, which is all that I am.

And armed thus with my past, and my future, and my present (which is a weapon, a weapon that takes whatever is available, a weapon bound to malice), they will mantle me, Oryx, the Taken King.

They will become me and I will become them, each of us defeating the other, correcting the other, alloying ourselves into one omnipotent philosophy. Thus I will live forever.

I'll make sure.

CHAPTER 2

The Burden of Light

If there is Light, there also must be Darkness.

One reveals the other. Tends it. Carves it like marble to reveal a new shape. There is a balance between them.

Therefore, to understand the Darkness we study the Light. Just as Light is connected through space and time, so is the Darkness. And, just as the Light has those who serve, who act as hands, and heart, and will, there are those who wield the Dark in the same fashion.

The Light healed us, and so we have a responsibility to give it back the lives it has given us. There will be a day when we meet a new kind of Guardian.

Light and Dark. Power and Weakness.
Guardian and Guardian.

Symmetry.

The Last Word

Once Was Palamon

I'm writing this from memory—some mine, but not all. The facts won't sync with the reality, but they'll be close, and there's no one to say otherwise, so for all intents and purposes, this will be the history of a settlement we called Palamon and the horrors that followed an all too brief peace.

I remember home, and stories of a paradise we'd all get to see some day—of a City, "shining even in the night." Palamon didn't shine, but it was sanctuary, of a sort.

We'd settled in the heart of a range that stretched the horizon. Wooded mountains that shot with purpose toward the sky. Winters were harsh, but the trees and peaks hid us from the world. We talked about moving on, sometimes, striking out for the City. But it was just a longing.

Drifters came and went. On occasion they would stay, but rarely. We had no real government, but there was rule of law. Basic tenets agreed upon by all and eventually overseen by Magistrate Loken.

And there you have it... no government, until there was. I was young, so I barely understood. I remember Loken as a hardworking man who just became broken. Mostly I think he was sad. Sad and frightened. As his fingers tightened on Palamon, people left. Those who stayed saw our days became grey. Loken's protection—from the Fallen, from ourselves—became dictatorial.

Looking back, I think maybe Loken had just lost too much—of himself, his family. But everyone lost something. And some of us had nothing to begin with. My only memory of my parents is a haze, like a daydream, and a small light, like the spark of their souls. It's not anything I dwell on. They left me early, taken by Dregs.

Palamon raised me from there. The family I call my own—called my own—cared for me as if I was their natural born son. And life was good. Being the only life I knew, my judgment is skewed, and it wasn't easy—pocked by loss as it was—but I would call it good.

Until, of course, it wasn't.

Until two men entered my world. One a light. The other the darkest shadow I would ever know.

The Last Word 2
The Weight of Truth

The man I would come to know as Jaren Ward, my third father and quite possibly my closest friend, came to Palamon from the south.

I was just a boy, but I'll never forget his silhouette on the empty trail as he made his slow walk into town.

I'd never seen anything like him. Maybe none of us had. He'd said he was only passing through, and I believed him—still do, but life can get in the way of intent, and often does.

I can picture that day with near perfect clarity. Of all the details though—every nuance, every moment—the memory that sticks in my mind is the iron on Jaren's hip. A cannon that looked both pristine and lived in. Like a relic of every battle he'd ever fought, hung low at his waist—a trophy and a warning.

This man was dangerous, but there was a light about him—a pureness to his weight—that seemed to hint that his ire was something earned, not carelessly given.

I'd been the first to see him as he approached, but soon most of Palamon had turned out to greet him. My father held me back as everyone stood in silence.

Jaren didn't make a sound behind his sleek racer's helmet. He looked just like the heroes in the stories, and to this day I'm not sure one way or the other if the silence between the town's people and the adventurer was born of fear or respect. I like to think the latter, but any truth I try to place on the moment would be of my own making.

As we waited for Magistrate Loken to arrive and make an official greeting, my patience got the best of me. I shook free of my father's heavy hand and made the short sprint across the court, stopping a few paces from where this new curiosity stood—a man unlike any other.

I stared up at him and he lowered his attention to me, his eyes hidden behind the thick tinted visor of his headgear. My sight quickly fell to his sidearm. I was transfixed by it. I imagined all the places that weapon had been. All of the wonders it had seen. The horrors it had endured. My imagination darted from one heroic act to the next.

I barely registered when he began to kneel, holding out the iron as if an offering. But my eyes locked onto the piece, mesmerized.

I recall turning back to my father and seeing the looks on the faces of everyone I knew. There was worry there—my father slowly shaking his head as if pleading with me to ignore the gift.

I turned back to the man I would come to know as Jaren Ward, the finest Hunter this system may ever know and one of the greatest Guardians to ever defend the Traveler's Light...

And I took the weapon in my hand. Carefully. Gently.

Not to use. But to observe. To imagine. To feel its weight and know its truth.

That was the first time I held "Last Word," but, unfortunately, not the last.

The Last Word

"Yours...not mine."

—Renegade Hunter Shin Malphur to Dredgen Yor
during the showdown at Dwindler's Ridge

The Last Word is a romantic weapon, a throwback
to simpler times when steady aim and large
rounds were enough to dispense justice in the
wilds of a lawless frontier. Of course, some might
say that time has come again.

The Dark Age 2
A Good Man's Deed

Loken's men found Jaren Ward in the courtyard where this had all began.

Nine guns trained on him. Nine cold hearts awaiting the order. Magistrate Loken, standing behind them, looked pleased with himself.

Jaren Ward stood in silence. His Ghost peeked out over his shoulder.

Loken took in the crowd before stepping forward, as if to claim the ground—his ground. "You question me?" There was venom in his words. "This is not your home."

I remember Loken's gestures here. Making a show of it all.

Everyone else was still. Quiet.

I tugged at my father's sleeve, but he just tightened his grip on my shoulder to the point of pain. His way of letting me know that this was not the time.

I'd watched Jaren's every move over the past months, mapping his effortless gestures and slight, earned mannerisms. I'd never seen anything like him. He was something I couldn't comprehend, and yet I felt I understood all I needed the moment I'd seen him. He was more than us. Not better. Not superior. Just more.

I wanted father to stop what was happening. Looking back now, I realize that he didn't want to stop it. No one did.

As Loken belittled Jaren Ward, taunted him, enumerated his crimes and sins, my eyes were stuck on Jaren's pistol, fixed to his hip. His steady hand resting calmly on his belt.

I remembered the pistol's weight. Effortless. And my concern faded. I understood.

"This is our town! My town!" Loken was shouting now. He was going to make a show of Jaren—teach the people of Palamon a lesson in obedience.

Jaren spoke: clear, calm. "Not anymore."

Loken laughed dismissively. He had nine guns on his side. "Those gonna be your last words then, boy?"

The movement was a flash: quick as chain lightning. Jaren Ward spoke as he moved. "Yours. Not mine."

Smoke trailed from Jaren's revolver.

Loken hit the ground. A dark hole in his forehead. Eyes staring into eternity.

Jaren stared down the nine guns trained on him. One by one, they lowered their aim. And the rest of my life began—where, in a few short years, so many others would be ended.

Thorn

The Rose

The noble man stood. And the people looked to him. For he was a beacon—hope given form, yet still only a man. And within that truth there was great promise. If one man could stand against the night, then so too could anyone—everyone.

In his strong hand the man held a Rose. And his aura burned bright.

When the man journeyed on, the people remembered. In his wake hope spread. But the man had a secret fear. His thoughts were dark. A sadness crept from the depths of his being. He had been a hero for so long, but pride had led him down sorrow's road.

Slowly the shadows' whisper became a voice, a dark call, offering glories enough to make even the brightest Light wander. He knew he was fading, yet he still yearned.

On his last day he sat and watched the sun fall. His final thoughts, pure of mind, if not body, held to a fleeting hope—though they would suffer for the man he would become, the people would remember him as he had been.

And so the noble man hid himself beneath a darkness no flesh should touch, and gave up his mortal self to claim a new birthright.

Whether this was choice, or destiny, is a truth known only to fate.

In that cool evening air, as dusk was devoured by night, the noble man ceased to exist. In his place another stood.

Same meat. Same bone. But so very different.

The first and only of his family. The sole forbearer and last descendent of the name Yor.

In his first moments as a new being, he looked down at his Rose and realized for the first time that it held no petals: only the jagged purpose of angry thorns.

Thorn

"To rend one's enemies is to see them not as equals, but objects—hollow of spirit and meaning."

—13th Understanding, 7th Book of Sorrow

Augmented through dark practices, Thorn was once a hero's weapon. Its jagged frame hints at a sinister truth: a powerful connection to the unutterable sorceries of the Hive.

The legend of Thorn is bound to the rise and fall of Dredgen Yor, a Guardian whose name is remembered with disgust and shame. The weapon was thought destroyed... but rumors of its existence still haunt the wilds.

Thorn 2
The Bloom

TYPE: Transcript.

DESCRIPTION: Conversation.

PARTIES: Four [4]. Three [3] unidentified [u.1, u.2, u.3], One [1] unconfirmed.

ASSOCIATIONS: Breaklands; Durga; Last Word; Malphur, Shin; North Channel; Palamon; Thorn; Velor; Ward, Jaren; WoS; Yor, Dredgen;

//AUDIO UNAVAILABLE//

//TRANSCRIPT FOLLOWS.../

[u.1:0.1] Can I see what you got there?

[silence]

[u.1:0.2] Yer cannon... can I see it?

[beat]

[u.2:0.1] I know you?

[beat]

[u.1:0.3] Not that I can say.

[u.2:0.2] And you wanna hold my piece?

[beat]

[u.1:0.4] Just that I never... seen one like it.

[beat]

[u.2:0.3] No, you haven't.

[u.1:0.5] Looks dangerous.

[u.2:0.4] Seems, maybe, that's the point.

[u.1:0.6] Suppose so.

[u.1:0.7] Can I see it?

[u.2:0.5] Not likely.

[silence]

[u.1:0.8] Where'd... where'd you find it?

[silence]

[u.1:0.9] You hearin' me?

[silence]

[u.3:0.1] He asked you question.

[silence]

[u.2:0.6] Didn't find it. Made it.

[u.1:1.0] Heh. Helluva touch you got then. You a 'smith?

[u.2:0.7] I look like a 'smith?

[u.1:1.1] Looks can be deceiving.

[u.2:0.8] Got that right.

[u.1:1.2] There a problem?

[u.2:0.9] Doesn't need to be.

[u.1:1.3] Glad we got that cleared up... Now, about that piece.

[silence]

[u.2:1.0] Been to Luna?

[u.1:1.4] Excuse me?

[u.2:1.1] The Moon. You been?

[u.1:1.5] Nobody's been.

[u.2:1.2] That a truth?

[u.1:1.6] That's a fact.

[u.2:1.3] Funny you'd make that distinction.

[u.1:1.7] Truth is you must think you're some kinda something special. With that attitude. The way you're just dismissin' us like we're nothing... like we ain't even here.

[u.1:1.8] Fact is... You ain't near as rock solid as you figure. Fact is, special's only special 'til it's not.

[silence]

[u.2:1.4] The bones say otherwise.

[u.1:1.9] Speak straight.

[u.2:1.5] You say "nobody." Bones say otherwise.

[u.1:2.0] What bones?

[u.2:1.6] All of them.

[u.1:2.1] What're you gettin' at?

[u.2:1.7] Too many to count.

[u.1:2.2] You trying to get a rile outta us? Was only making conversation.

[u.2:1.8] You really weren't.

[u.4:0.1] We got a smart one here.

[u.2:1.9] Experienced more than smart. But experience has its advantages.

[u.1:2.3] Experience tell you to lip off to strangers just tryin' to make talk?

[u.2:2.0] Keep insisting and maybe we will.

[u.1:2.4] Talk?

[u.2:2.1] Have words.

[u.1:2.5] Ain't that what we're doin'?

[u.2:2.2] My conversations tend to be a bit louder.

[silence]

[u.1:2.6] That a threat.

[u.2:2.3] A truth.

[u.1:2.7] Who the hell you think you are?

[u.2:2.4] According to your facts, "nobody." Yet, here I sit.

[u.1:2.8] Don't matter much how pretty yer cannon is. You keep it up, we'll see just how loud you like to get.

[silence]

[u.1:2.9] You done talkin' now? Guess he knows his place, boys.

[u.2:2.5] Ever have a nightmare?

[u.1:3.0] You playin' games? Or just thick?

[u.2:2.6] I know you have. This world? Can't help, but.

[u.1:3.1] I don't have nightmares. I give 'em.

[u.2:2.7] You are a goddamn cliché. The picture perfect bandit.

[u.2:2.8] Hearing your voice—the things you're saying, the shade of the hard man you pretend to be...

[u.1:3.2] Ain't no shade.

[audible crack]

[audible crack]

[audible crack]

[silence]

[u.2:2.8] Sit down.

[silence]

[u.2:3.0] Sit. Down.

[u.2:3.1] Your mouth just got your friends dead.

[u.2:3.2] This is what happens when you bore me. And right now...

[u.2:3.3] I'm so very bored.

[u.1:3.3] Wha... No listen...

[u.2:3.4] Shhhhh.

[u.1:3.4] But... but... you're a... you're one of them... A Guardian, right?

[u.1:3.5] You're supposed t'be one'a the good ones.

[u.2:3.5] "Supposed to be?" Maybe I am. Maybe this is what "good" looks like.

[u.2:3.6] Anymore, who can tell?

[u.1:3.6] I...

[u.2:3.7] You wanted to see my prize.

[u.1:3.7] No... I...

[u.2:3.8] Look at it.

[u.1:3.8] I...

[audible sobbing]

[u.2:3.9] Whimpering won't stop what comes next.

[u.2:4.0] Look...

[audible sobbing]

[u.2:4.1] Look at it.

[u.2:4.2] Open your eyes.

[audible sobbing]

[u.2:4.3] Not many get such a clean view.

[u.2:4.4] The bone... You see it. Jagged, like thorns.

[u.2:4.5] I used to think of it as a rose...

[u.2:4.6] Focusing on its bloom.

[u.2:4.7] But the bloom is just a byproduct of its anger.

[silence]

[u.2:4.8] You have nightmares?

[audible sobbing]

[u.2:4.9] Ever seen a nightmare? Ever opened your eyes and realized the horror wasn't a dream? The terror wasn't gone?

[u.2:5.0] I've seen nightmares.

[u.2:5.1] They live in the shadows.

[u.2:5.2] They've been watching.

[u.2:5.3] I thought... It's foolish, I know... but I thought I saw a way.

[u.2:5.4] That maybe we could win. Maybe we could survive.

[u.2:5.5] But once you step into those shadows, it's so very hard to walk in the Light.

[u.2:5.6] Or... maybe I just wasn't strong enough.

[u.2:5.7] Maybe.

[u.2:5.8] But I feel strong now. [audible sobbing]

[u.2:5.9] I stole the dark.

[u.2:6.0] Or, maybe it stole me.

[u.2:6.1] Either way, here we are.

[u.2:6.2] And I'm hungry.

[u.2:6.3] Its hungry.

[u.2:6.4] You have no Light beyond the spark of your pathetic life.

[u.2:6.5] But a spark is something.

[audible sobbing]

[u.2:6.6] Open your eyes.

[audible sobbing]

[audible sobbing]

[audible crack]

[silence]

[silence]

[silence]

/...END TRANSCRIPT///

Thorn 3

A Farewell to Light

TYPE: Transcript.

DESCRIPTION: Conversation.

PARTIES: Two [2]. One [1] Ghost-type, designate [REDACTED] [u.1], One [1] Guardian-type, Class [REDACTED] [u.2]

ASSOCIATIONS: [REDACTED]; Breaklands; Durga; Last Word; Malphur, Shin; North Channel; Palamon; Thorn; Velor; Ward, Jaren; WoS; Yor, Dredgen;

//AUDIO UNAVAILABLE//

//TRANSCRIPT FOLLOWS.../

[u.1:0.1] You were not always this man.

[u.2:0.1] True.

[u.1:0.2] Then the math says you do not need to remain this man. You can be other.

[u.2:0.2] I am other.

[u.1:0.3] You can be better.

[u.2:0.3] This is better.

[u.1:0.4] That matter, at best, is subjective.

[u.2:0.4] Then what? Lesser.

[u.1:0.5] Some would say.

[u.2:0.5] But what would you say?

[silence]

[u.2:0.6] All we've seen and now, here with me, you have no words.

[u.1:0.6] I have words.

[u.2:0.7] But...?

[u.1:0.7] But you will not like them.

[u.2:0.8] There is much I do not like.

[u.1:0.8] More now than ever it would seem.

[u.2:0.9] Heh.

[u.1:0.9] I find no laughing matter in your path.

[u.2:1.0] Only in the journey.

[u.1:1.0] What brought you here was nobility.

[u.2:1.1] And my prize.

[u.1:1.1] That is no prize.

[u.2:1.2] A curse then?

[u.1:1.2] I would say.

[u.2:1.3] And I would disagree.

[u.1:1.3] You are no longer yourself.

[u.2:1.4] I am myself. It's who I was that's gone.

[u.1:1.4] Who you were held all the value.

[u.2:1.5] To you.

[u.1:1.5] To the Light.

[u.2:1.6] The Light...

[u.1:1.6] It is all.

[u.2:1.7] It is nothing but a crutch.

[u.1:1.7] One that has held you up.

[u.2:1.8] Only just. And nothing more.

[u.1:1.8] Nothing more? You were a hero.

[u.2:1.9] And yet people still die. Corruption still exists. Light still fades. And Darkness still spreads.

[u.1:1.9] As it will ever be, that doesn't mean you give in to...

[u.2:2.0] To what? Hope.

[u.1:2.0] This is not hope.

[u.2:2.1] This is peace.

[u.1:2.1] You have blood on your hands.

[u.2:2.2] How's that any different than prior?

[u.1:2.2] Innocent blood.

[u.2:2.3] Matter of perspective.

[u.1:2.3] That's the shadow talking.

[u.2:2.4] And am I not.

[u.1:2.4] The shadow?

[u.2:2.5] Ya know... These past cycles, you've made an honorable effort. Tried your best to correct my course. But I don't know it needs correcting.

[u.1:2.5] And if it does?

[u.2:2.6] Could be too late.

[u.1:2.6] 'Could be' is a winding path.

[u.2:2.7] Long way from where I was to where I'm going.

[u.1:2.7] That is my hope. That there is still time.

[u.2:2.8] For?

[u.1:2.8] Corrective measures. The righting of our path. The cleansing of your shadow and a return to the Light.

[silence]

[u.2:2.9] Why'd you pick me?

[u.1:2.9] It doesn't work that way.

[u.2:3.0] Was I special?

[u.1:3.0] You were.

[u.2:3.1] But only as special as any other.

[u.1:3.1] You are all special.

[u.2:3.2] Seems to contradict the word don't it.

[u.1:3.2] Not in my estimation.

[u.2:3.3] If we're all special, are any of us special?

[u.1:3.3] Is that what you want? To be special?

[u.2:3.4] Heh.

[u.1:3.4] You dismiss, but it's a very serious question. Is that all you're after? Is all of the death worth that badge?

[u.2:3.5] Am I not already more than the rest?

[u.1:3.5] Looking at you here, now. The smoke, ash and bone at your feet mark you as so much less.

[u.2:3.6] Maybe. And yet here you are.

[u.1:3.6] Meaning?

[u.2:3.7] You have been at my side every step of the way.

[u.1:3.7] Where else would I be?

[u.2:3.8] Yet you disagree so thoroughly with my change in perspective.

[u.1:3.8] If only the change was simply one of perspective. Your "evolution" was no choice. This is not you having come to an understanding after careful considered thought. This is corruption.

[u.2:3.9] The shadows?

[u.1:3.9] The Darkness.

[u.2:4.0] Maybe so.

[u.1:4.0] There is no maybe here.

[u.2:4.1] And you think you can save me?

[u.1:4.1] I rekindled your Light, it falls first to me to aid in its survival.

[silence]

[u.2:4.2] I tire of it.

[u.1:4.2] You must try...

[u.2:4.3] I tire of you.

[u.1:4.3] [REDACTED]...

[u.2:4.4] That is no longer my name.

[u.1:4.4] I will not speak the other.

[u.2:4.5] It doesn't matter. This is where we part ways.

[u.1:4.5] I will not leave you.

[u.2:4.6] I am leaving you.

[u.1:4.6] Without me, your journey ahead will be more than any one Guardian can handle.

[u.2:4.7] That's the point. It's been sometime since you saw me as worthy of walking among those I once called brother and sister. Yet... anymore, I feel as though I am worthy of so much more.

[u.1:4.7] Without me... You will die.

[u.2:4.8] Someday. Won't be the first time.

[silence]

[u.2:4.9] Consider this my last good deed. I am releasing you of the burden of my deeds, both done and yet to come.

[u.1:4.8] I will not abandon you.

[u.2:5.0] You will. Or I will carve the Light from your shell and leave the carcass of my first and last friend in the dirt of this dull, red world for no one to find.

[u.1:4.9] Then I've failed you, completely.

[u.2:5.1] Not me. Maybe the man I was.

[u.1:5.0] He is truly dead.

[u.2:5.2] I believe so.

[u.1:5.1] Belief is not fact.

[u.2:5.3] Semantics I no longer have the patience for.

[silence]

[u.2:5.4] When you speak of me, use my proper name. Tell them of the man that stands before you, not the ghost of the hero I once was.

[u.1:5.2] You will always be [REDACTED] to me.

[u.2:5.5] If you cannot let that man go, you will forever taint his legacy. All the good I have ever done will be washed away in the fire of who I have become.

[u.1:5.3] If you care, there is still some promise within you.

[u.2:5.6] If I am being honest, I care only to give hope to the frightened, huddled masses so that when I come upon them they will have more to lose. Their pain will be greater. Their screams more pure.

[u.1:5.4] You...

[u.2:5.7] Nothing dies like hope. I cherish it.

[u.1:5.5] You're a monster.

[u.2:5.8] Finally, you see the truth.

[u.1:5.6] [REDACTED] is truly dead.

[u.2:5.9] So I've said. Long live Dredgen Yor.

[u.1:5.7] This is farewell, but you can only run from your sins so far. In the end, you will die alone.

[u.2:6.0] Maybe so. But I gotta tell ya... I tend to like my odds.

[u.1:5.8] Your tainted "Rose" will not always save you.

[u.2:6.1] Old friend... It already has.

/...END TRANSCRIPT///

The Last Word 3
Long Roads, Dead Ends

It was the fourth night of the seventh moon.

Nine rises since any sign.

Trail wasn't cold, but lukewarm would've been an exaggeration.

Jaren had us hold by a ravine.

The heavy wood along the cliff's edge caught the wind, holding back the cold and the rush of water muffled our conversation.

We'd seen dual Skiffs hanging low as they cut through the valley.

Wasn't known Fallen territory, but anymore that's a dangerous assumption.

There were six of us then.

Three less than two moons prior, but still, one more than when we'd first turned our backs to Palamon's ash.

We took a rotation for watch during the night.

Movement was kept to a minimum and communication was down to hand signals and simple gestures.

We could hold our own in a fight, but only the dead went looking for one—a hard truth that cut in direct opposition to our reasons for being so far from anything resembling civilization, much less our safety.

The Skiffs had spooked Kressler and Nada, and, in truth, me as well. But, looking back, I think we were all just grasping for any good reason to turn back.

Not because we would—turn back—but because it seemed to be our only real hope, and I think we all knew it.

Forward. Where we were headed—into the unknown. And following the footsteps we were. It all just started to feel like a never-ending dead end after a while.

Jaren never wavered though. Not once.

At least not to any noticeable degree.

It was his drive, his conviction, that kept us going.

And—it's hard to think on—but if I'm honest, it was his death that rekindled my own fire. A fire that was all but exhausted on that cold night.

He seemed confident we were close.

But more than confident—sure. He seemed sure.

No one else felt it—our own confidence, and any enthusiasm we'd had was set to wither soon as Brevin, Trenn and Mel were gunned down.

The Ghost—Jaren's Ghost—never said a word to any of us. Just hung there. Always alert. Always judging. Not us, per se, but the moment. Any moment.

I never got the sense it thought of us as lesser. More that it was guarded, wary.

We knew it could speak. We'd overheard them a few times. Just brief words, and no one ever pressed the subject.

From time to time I caught its gaze lingering on me, but always assumed the attention was a result of the bond Jaren and I had. He was a father to me. At the time I didn't know why he'd singled me out as someone to care for. Someone to protect. After all the loss, I welcomed it, but looking back—taking in the arm's length at which he kept the others—I guess I should've known, or at least suspected there was more to it.

We all woke that night, closer to morning than the previous day.

A crack of gunfire split through the wood. Then more.

Far off, but near enough to pump the blood.

A familiar ring. "Last Word." Jaren's sidearm. His best friend. Then another. A single shot, an unmistakable echo calling through the night. Hushed, cutting.

One shot, dark and infernal. Followed by silence.

We crouched low and quiet. Listening. Hoping.

Jaren was gone. Off on his own.

Maybe we were closer than we'd allowed ourselves to believe.

Too close.

He'd gone to face death alone.

I couldn't admit it—not at the time—but he thought he was protecting us.

After such a long road—years on its heels, a trail littered with suffering and fire—maybe he just couldn't take the thought of anymore dead "kids," as he called us.

The echoes faded and we all held still. No way to track the direction. No sense in rushing blind.

What was done was done.

The cadence of the shots fired told a story none of us cared to hear.

"Last Word" it hadn't been. And somewhere in the world, close enough for us to bear absent witness but far enough to be a dream, Jaren Ward lay dead or dying. And there was nothing to be done.

Hours passed. An eternity.

We held our spot, but as the sun rose the others began to fade back into the world. Without Jaren there was nothing holding us together. No driving force. Vengeance had grown stale as a motivator. Fear and a longing to see more suns rise drove a wedge between duty and desire.

By midday I was alone. I couldn't leave. Wouldn't.

Either I would find Jaren and set him at ease, or the other would find me and that would be a fitting end.

Death marching on.

But then, a motion. Quick and darting. My muscles tensed and my hand shot to the grip of my leadslinger.

Then a confirmation of the horrible truth I had already accepted, as Jaren's Ghost came to a halt a few paces in front of me.

I exhaled and slumped forward. Still standing, but broken. The tiny Light looked me over with a curious tilt to its axis, then shot a beam of light over my body. Scanning me as it had done the very first time we met.

I looked up. Staring into its singular glowing eye.

And it spoke...

Thorn 4

The Shadow and the Light

TYPE: Transcript.

DESCRIPTION: Conversation.

PARTIES: Two [2]. One [1] Ghost-type, designate [REDACTED] [u.1], One [1] Guardian-type, Class [REDACTED] [u.2]

ASSOCIATIONS: Breaklands; Durga; Dwindler's Ridge; Last Word; Malphur, Shin; North Channel; Palamon; Thorn; Velor; Ward, Jaren; WoS; Yor, Dredgen;

//AUDIO UNAVAILABLE//

//TRANSCRIPT FOLLOWS.../

[u.1:0.1] Such Darkness.

[u.2:0.1] Impressed?

[u.1:0.2] Far from it.

[u.2:0.2] To each their own.

[u.1:0.3] His Light is faded.

[u.2:0.3] His Light is gone.

[u.1:0.4] You are an infection.

[u.2:0.4] I am that which will cleanse.

[u.1:0.5] You are a monster.

[u.2:0.5] Heh. An old friend once saw me as the same. He was right, and, had we met earlier, so too would you be.

[u.1:0.6] You'd dare defend yourself—all you've done—as anything but monstrous?

[u.2:0.6] No more than a hurricane.

[u.1:0.7] Then you're a force of nature?

[u.2:0.7] I am all that is right. You may not see it—for lack of looking, or blind ignorance—but I am all that is good.

[u.1:0.8] You've just murdered a good man.

[u.2:0.8] He shot first.

[u.1:0.9] Yet you stand.

[u.2:0.9] Guess he missed.

[u.1:1.0] He never misses.

[u.2:1.0] First time for everything.

[silence]

[u.2:1.1] His cannon? Nice piece of hardware.

[u.2:1.2] Well-worn, but clean. Smooth hammer.

[u.1:1.1] It was his prize.

[u.2:1.3] Guess he put too much faith in the wrong steel.

[u.1:1.2] Is that where your faith lies, in steel?

[u.2:1.4] Not for some time. My steel is only an extension. My faith is in the shadow.

[u.1:1.3] Then my Light is an affront to all you are. I am your truest enemy.

[u.2:1.5] One of many.

[u.1:1.4] Would you end me?

[u.2:1.6] Not you. Not now.

[u.1:1.5] The shadow knows mercy.

[u.2:1.7] The shadow knows no such thing.

[u.1:1.6] Then what?

[u.2:1.8] The other.

[u.1:1.7] What other?

[u.2:1.9] The dead man's charge.

[u.1:1.8] The boy?

[u.1:1.9] You'd end him as well?

[u.2:2.0] If it comes to that... We'll see.

[u.1:2.0] I won't let you have the child.

[u.2:2.1] Been long enough now, think maybe he's a man.

[u.1:2.1] You cannot have him.

[u.2:2.2] Not yet.

[u.1:2.2] I won't let you.

[u.2:2.3] That you could stop me is an amusing thought.

[silence]

[u.2:2.4] Here.

[silence]

[u.2:2.5] Take it.

[u.1:2.3] Why?

[u.2:2.6] Give the apprentice his master's "sword." It is a gift.

[u.1:2.4] You cannot have him.

[u.2:2.7] You fear for his Light?

[u.1:2.5] He...

[u.2:2.8] ...is special.

[u.1:2.6] Yes.

[u.2:2.9] I am aware.

[u.1:2.7] You're trying to tempt him. You're feeding his anger.

[u.2:3.0] The gun is a memento, nothing more.

[u.1:2.8] You claim to be a vessel, a hollow shell where once a man stood, but that is just a lie. The man is still in you.

[u.2:3.1] There is no man here, I am now, and for the rest of time, only Dredgen Yor.

[u.1:2.9] "The Eternal Abyss?"

[u.2:3.2] So, not all the forgotten languages are dead.

[u.1:3.0] Hide behind whatever titles you wish, it is all still a façade. No force of nature would play such games.

[u.2:3.3] Games?

[u.1:3.1] The cannon. You wish to tempt the boy. To spur him on and fuel his rage. There is intent there. The actions of a man, monstrous, mad or otherwise... you are nothing more.

[u.2:3.4] And what value does your conclusion bring, flawed as it may be?

[u.1:3.2] That a hurricane can only be weathered, not stopped. Not redirected. A force of nature is uncaring and without intent, but a man...

[u.2:3.5] Yes?

[u.1:3.3] A man is none of those things.

[silence]

[u.1:3.4] A man can be killed.

[silence]

[u.2:3.6] And there it is...

[u.1:3.5] There what is...?

[u.2:3.7] A sliver of hope.

The Last Word 4

Showdown at Dwindler's Ridge

Then.

Palamon was ash.

I was only a boy—my face caked in soot, snot and sorrow.

I'd assumed Jaren, my friend, our Guardian, the savior of Palamon, would always protect us—could always save us...

But I was a fool.

Jaren, and the others, only a handful, but still our best hunters, our hardest hearts, had left three suns prior. Tracking Fallen, after the bandits had caused a stir.

The stranger—the other—arrived the following day.

He rarely spoke. Took a room. Took our hospitality.

I was intrigued by him, as I was Jaren when he'd first arrived.

But the stranger was cold. Distant. Damaged, I thought.

But I wasn't afraid. Not yet.

Only a child, I knew the monsters of our world to walk like men, but they were not. They were something alien. Four-armed and savage.

The stranger was polite, but solemn.

I took him for a sad, broken man, and he was. Though, at the time, I didn't understand how that could make one dangerous.

As with Jaren, father made an effort to keep me away from the stranger.

It wouldn't matter.

As the silhouette approached, fear held tight.

The dark figure towered over me. Looking into me—through me.

He smiled. My knees weak. All lost.

Then, he turned and walked away.

Leaving ruin and a heartbroken, terrified boy in his wake without a second glance.

I've been chasing that stranger's shadow ever since.

Now.

We stood silent, the sun high.

Seconds passed, feeling more like hours.

He looked different.

He seemed, now, to be weightless—effortless in an existence that would crush a man burdened by conscience.

My gaze remained locked as I felt a heat rising inside of me. The other spoke...

"Been awhile."

I gave no reply.

"The gunslinger's sword... his cannon. That was a gift."

My silence held as my thumb caressed the perfectly worn hammer at my hip.

"An offering from me... to you."

The heat grew. Centered in my chest.

I felt like a coward the day Jaren Ward died and for many cycles after.

But here, I felt only the fire of my Light.

The other probed...

"Nothing to say?"

He let the words hang.

"I've been waiting for you. For this day."

His attempt at conversation felt mundane when judged against all that had come before.

"Many times I thought you'd faltered. Given up..."

All I'd lost, all who'd suffered, flashed rapid through my mind, intercut with a dark silhouette walking toward a frightened, weak, coward of a boy.

The fire burned in me.

The other continued...

"But here you are. This is truly an end..."

As his tongue slipped between syllables my gun hand moved as if of its own will.

Reflex and purpose merged with anger, clarity and an overwhelming need for just that... an end.

In step with my motion, the fire within burst into focus—through my shoulder, down my arm—as my finger closed on the trigger of my third father's cannon.

Two shots. Two bullets engulfed in an angry glow.

The other fell.

I walked to his corpse. He never raised his cursed Thorn—the jagged gun with the festering sickness.

I looked down at the dead man who had caused so much death.

My shooter still embraced by the dancing flames of my Light.

A sadness came over me.

I thought back to my earliest days. Of Palamon. Of Jaren.

Leveling my cannon at the dead man's helm, I paid one final tribute to my mentor, my savior, my father and my friend...

"Yours... Not mine."

...as I closed my grip, allowing Jaren's cannon, now my own, to have the last, loud word.

Rezyl Azzir
Before These Walls

Rezyl Azzir was a man.

In time his kind would be called Titan. Mountains of muscle and might and metal. His collar was fur and teeth. His person clad in ornate, golden-etched plating, trophies upon his shoulders.

This was before the City was The City.

This is before the walls. Still in the shadow of the fragile giant above, but before.

Salvation seekers came—survivors; weary remnants of a people on the brink.

These were the days before reason took hold. Before study was merged with belief.

The giant was looked to as one would a God. Maybe it still is.

Factions grew from the huddled masses. Like minds coming together to provide support, comfort. Over time these loyalties demanded loyalty. Differences that used to inform—viewpoints that when joined granted a larger understanding of the whole—became points of conflict. The sanctuary became divided. The shadow of Light grew darker. This, humanity's last oasis, slowly fading to a mirage.

Great, powerful men and women, The Risen, stood at the Factions' sides.

Protection. Enforcers. Misused possibility.

Misery crept into this false paradise. Yet hope lingered.

Seeing the cracks in this society born beneath the giant's fractured shell, some among The Risen challenged the dissolution of all that could be. They would no longer serve as instruments of oppression. They would be more.

Thus began an unnecessary war made necessary by greed, ambition... fear. And, in the chaos of this struggle, came the scavengers—aliens with appetites. A common enemy.

In the end, the scavengers were repelled and the Factions fell, their grip broken, though their beliefs remained. This was the earliest days of the Guardians, when might found purpose. Prosperity was in reach.

Rezyl had been a champion of these wars. A leader. Against the alien pirates he had been more. If the giant wasn't a God, then maybe Rezyl was.

As the first walls formed—built of hard work and sacrifice—Rezyl and the Guardians stood against the alien plunderers time and again. More survivors arrived. More warriors.

The Guardian ranks swelled.

The City grew.

Hope blossomed. To Rezyl it was a currency. Hope bought tomorrow. Tomorrow bought the effort needed to survive today.

Yet Rezyl grew weary. Stories haunted his nights. Old stories. Those no longer told. Those locked behind tight lips for fear of what they may invoke. Whenever the sun dropped below the horizon and the moon rose high, Rezyl's thoughts wandered. How safe was safe? How long could they fight with the Darkness still writhing?

So, every day Rezyl would fight and build and protect. And every day a city grew beneath the giant. And every night he would think about all that was never said and stare intently at the moon above.

Rezyl Azzir

War Without End

— Eksori's Ambush —

His foot pressed hard to the sun-cracked ground. Beneath it the Vandal's neck gave; a hiss of ether burst free before dissipating.

Rezyl turned. Three Dregs charged. Their Captain raised his shock blade high, unleashing a battle cry to fuel their courage.

Focused fire spit from the muzzle of Rezyl's full-auto. The Dregs fell.

To the Captain, Rezyl was a trophy that would buy unmatched respect among his Devil brothers.

To Rezyl, the Captain was already an afterthought. As ether leaked from the pirate's broken body with each blow of Rezyl's heavy fists, Rezyl's attention had shifted to the unknown, but inevitable, battles to follow.

This was the state of things; conflict as common as breath.

— The Tescan Valley Encounter —

A Ketch with unfamiliar markings hung low between two peaks. A rare sight. Fallen flagships weren't known to linger so close to the surface, preferring constant motion, like sharks on the hunt.

Skiffs circled below the Ketch as their crews pre-pared to plunder any treasures the facility held.

Rezyl leveled his rocket launcher. A digital ping signaled a lock, and a trail of smoke shot toward the lead Skiff.

Two more rockets followed in rapid succession.

The lead Skiff took two hits, lurched and retreated back toward the Ketch above.

The third rocket caught a trailing Skiff as the craft turned to engage its attackers.

Rezyl looked back. "Go."

"You can't take a Ketch alone," Hassa laughed.

"The ship isn't my target," Rezyl had a plan. Hassa hated Rezyl's plans with equal parts envy and concern.

"Lead the Skiffs away," he continued. "We'll meet— "

"Can't meet if you're dead," Tover shot back.

Rezyl smiled beneath his helm, "Go."

Hassa and Tover throttled their Sparrows and disappeared into the heavy woods. Rezyl watched from cover as the Skiffs gave chase.

The Fallen below had taken defensive positions. The rocket attack caught them off guard but they were ready now, and there were more of them than he had time to count.

Rezyl raced down the slope, weaving between the thick growth of brush and pine, on a direct path for the Fallen clustered at the mountain's base, his Ghost at his side.

"I need you to hang back."

"Uhhh..."

"Trust me."

"Always have."

"How quick can you light my spark?"

"You expect to die? Can't say that's the best—"

"How quick?"

"Quick."

"Be ready."

"For?"

"You'll know."

Rezyl's Ghost slowed as the Guardian hit the valley floor.

The Fallen opened fire.

Rezyl leapt from his Sparrow as it transmatted away, his rifle spraying lead at the entrenched pirates.

The Fallen's Arc bolts peppered Rezyl. Eager Dregs rushed and were met with death as Rezyl marched forward.

A massive blast cratered the ground a few feet from the Titan. The Ketch had turned its guns on Rezyl.

Another blast impacted to Rezyl's left and he stumbled. A third exploded directly in his path...

...and Rezyl fell.

From the treeline, his Ghost watched as the Fallen celebrated and a Skiff drifted down from the Ketch above.

The circle around Rezyl's body parted and the imposing figure of their Kell stepped forward to admire his prize.

The chittering excitement quieted to a steady drone as the Kell lifted Rezyl's limp body by the neck.

A chorus rose among the crew, growing louder as the Kell hefted Rezyl over his head for all to see.

Rezyl's Ghost darted low through the crowd. He didn't like Rezyl's plan, but now he understood it.

Distracted by their Kell's triumph, the Ghost's presence went unnoticed until a beam of light swept over Rezyl's body.

The mood shifted instantly, cheers turning to ravenous shouts.

The Kell's gaze fell to the Ghost as the beam faded.

The circle began to collapse — the Fallen set to pounce.

As the Kell moved to toss Rezyl aside, cold steel met the underside of the alien marauder's jaw, followed by a red flash as Rezyl pulled his cannon's trigger.

Ether spewed in an angry geyser and the Kell's grip loosened. Rezyl hit the ground and unloaded five more rounds into the Fallen leader's torso. The monster dropped.

Frenzied, the Kell's crew closed in like a flood.

Rezyl's Ghost lifted above the fray, frantic, "Now! Now! Now!"

In one motion, Rezyl rose from a crouch, his fists clenched and raised high as a storm of Arc Light built within him, his full might raining down on the Kell's chest. The shockwave of Rezyl's attack hit like a meteor, shatteringthe Kell's body and any Fallen within the Havoc storm's radius.

The remaining Fallen staggered, knocked back and dazed.

Rezyl triggered his Sparrow.

His Ghost flew to his side, "We leaving?"

"Before that Ketch opens up on us."

Rezyl punched the throttle as the Fallen crew opened fire.

"Let's never do that again," his Ghost pleaded.

Rezyl didn't have to reply. If war was a constant, "never" was just an illusion.

— In Defense of North Channel —

Winds from the south caught the smoke and began to clear the thick air.

Slowly, the citizens of the small, snow-covered settlement came out from their hiding places.

Rezyl surveyed their faces—each weary, but flecked with hope.

Living in the wilds was all they had known. Surviving. Fighting. Hiding. These people had heard stories of a safer place, but tales of a better life were so rarely true.

Rezyl and his companions had been tracking these. Fallen for weeks. Had they caught them sooner this town would have been spared. That any survivors climbed from the rubble to see another day marked this as a victory, but Rezyl was growing tired of small wins, however meaningful.

That evening, Rezyl and the others led a gathering of survivors on the long journey to the growing city beneath the Traveler. Some settlers remained behind, choosing to stake their claim in the untamed wilds.

Rezyl admired their resolve, but never looked back. He knew whatever death these brave pioneers avoided that day would come to them... someday... in one form or another.

Rezyl Azzir

The Whisper and the Bone

Something in Rezyl was telling him he shouldn't be here.

Something deep.

Something resembling fear.

He knelt, examining the dust-covered pile at his feet.

The skulls had been discarded with little care some time ago—decades, maybe longer.

The doors carved into the rock face were arcane—dark, gothic... other... and large.

The jagged finery of their archway spoke to an artistry that only served to strengthen the sinking feeling in his gut.

Rezyl had come to Luna in search of nightmares, and after his long journey— from the growing City beneath the Traveler to the ends of the Earth and beyond— he found himself face-to-face with the remnants of stories he'd hoped were nothing but lies.

He stood, a large man made small against the massive, looming doorway.

The knot in his stomach was telling him to turn back.

Instead, he moved forward, toward the doors; sealed, as they were, for ages untold.

After only a few steps, a shrill, heavy scraping cut the air.

The massive doors were opening.

Rezyl steadied his rifle as a lone shape, floating just above the ground, appeared from the deep black beyond the threshold.

The figure in the doorway—a dark, ethereal woman cloaked in tattered ceremony and armored with ornate bone— danced in the air.

Rezyl and the demon woman held their ground, contemplating one another.

With no warning the silent intimacy of the moment was broken by a booming, angry call from deep within the doorway. The sound, thick and pained, echoed across the narrow valley then fell silent.

After a beat that felt like eternity, the figure backed away into the dark.

The doors remained wide—an invitation or a dare, Rezyl did not know. Nor did he care.

The mighty Titan took steps forward. "Uhhhh... I'm not sure this is a good idea," his Ghost's concern was impossible to mistake.

"Not sure that matters."

"We've come. We've seen. Maybe the best course here is to warn others. Gather an army."

"Maybe."

"I'm just saying... It's possible you can't handle whatever it is we've upset here."

"We've woken nightmares." Rezyl's attention was singular; focused intently on the dark beyond the threshold.

"The Hive were supposed to be gone." The Ghost mulled the full consequence of this mistaken belief. "They've been silent for—"

"They're not silent anymore."

"That scream? These doors? They're best left alone."

"I can't do that."

Rezyl continued forward. Toward the dark. Toward the unknown.

"Stay here."

"Excuse me?"

"Get distance. We don't know what this is... what's coming. Can't risk you too close to an unknown."

"And if you fall where I can't find you?"

"If I fall... If I don't return. Run. Tell the others. Warn them all... There are worse things than pirates."

Rezyl steadied his rifle and stepped into the dark, as his Ghost lingered.

—

Hours passed. More? Time was lost in this place, and with it any remembrance of hope... of promise... of purpose in the longing for a brighter tomorrow.

Down amongst the shadows there were no tomorrows.

Down in the abyss there was no hope.

Rezyl's footfalls echoed; lonely, measured steps with no guarantee of purchase. At any moment the world could fall away and he would be lost—the forgotten hero who foolishly sought nightmares.

Then, a presence. Sweeping and dream-like.

Rezyl leveled his rifle.

He could sense the witch, but found it impossible to track her in the dark.

Rezyl opened fire. Short, focused bursts to light the ebony corridor.

The demon witch circled just beyond the reach of each burst's glow.

Rezyl kept firing, using the short flickers of light to gain bearing.

The witch laughed and a thick black cloud engulfed Rezyl.

The Titan kept firing but his movements were restricted. The cloud confined him, caged him.

He could hear her moving just beyond his sight as her laughter rose in pitch, cutting into Rezyl's mind and soul like a tempered blade.

Rezyl flinched as the wicked woman began to speak in a tongue that resembled torture more than language.

The pain was searing, complete.

The demon approached the writhing hero.

As she spoke her violent words began to take shape, morphing from syllables of death to a known offering of haunted human languages.

The demon woman leaned in close... and whispered, intimately.

Rezyl's ears bled as she spoke.

"I am the end of 'morrows. Xyor, the Blessed. Xyor, the Betrothed. I am of the coming storm. These are not my words, but prophesy. Your Light will one day shatter and die. For now it simply offends... And you, dear, sweet, fragile thing, shall be made to suffer for your transgressions upon this holy ground."

As the witch fell silent, her hateful voice was replaced by a growing chorus of hungry, manic chittering and the rising thunder of an approaching flood.

Rezyl had come looking for the terrors that hide just beyond the light.

He found them.

Or, maybe...

...they found him.

Rezyl Azzir

The Triumphant Fall

The trigger clicked.

Another empty clip slid from its purchase and dropped to the dark stone floor.

It was the last.

His rifle was dry.

Rezyl spun the weapon in his hand, grabbing hard around the barrel, like a club.

A new wave of chittering death was upon him—fragile but aggressive, overwhelming in their number and oppressive in their rage.

The stock of the rifle connected with skull after skull.

They caved and fell.

Like the others before.

The pile of vanquished nightmares—half bone, half dust—grew at Rezyl's feet.

There was a calm to him. An ease.

The chaos of battle was no time to panic.

His swing was wide, but measured. No wasted movement.

A demon clawed at his back. Then another.

They were heavier than their frail frames would suggest.

He gave a shrug and shake, turned and hammered the stock hard into the side of one creature's temple. Its skull splintered and the stock lodged deep in the wet, chalky mass beneath the bone. He made a fleeting effort to break the rifle free, but had to let it fall away as the rush of demons increased.

Rezyl kicked the other monster to the floor, stepping on its neck while shifting to backhand a throng of attackers eager to make their killing lunge.

If the rifle—his battle-worn Inferno—had served to thin the herd and buy Rezyl time to assess the whole of the situation, his Rose would see him through.

It always had.

The Titan, awash in the ash and gore of his enemies, pulled his cannon and in one motion feathered the trigger to level the wretched beasts closest to him.

The bloom from each shot lit the cavern with flashes of red heat—a garden of angry roses blossoming in pointed defiance of this vile, hateful kingdom of shadows.

On the far end of the sea of gnashing maws, the wicked woman danced in the air.

Watching.

Waiting?

Rezyl's cannon was loaded and ready to fire as if an afterthought.

He let loose another barrage and six more demons slumped, lifeless upon the pile.

The witch unleashed a violent cry.

And as quickly as it had begun, the onslaught subsided.

The chittering fell from a deafening roar to an eerie chorus humming through the ebon haze just beyond his sight.

Rezyl stood, straightened his tired back and took long, deep breaths.

The storm had not been weathered.

He could feel it in his gut.

He stood now, not at peace, but within the eye—the swirling, terrible lull before the waves came crashing once more.

The wicked woman laughed: a horrid, grating screech.

Followed by footsteps. Heavy and hard.

Thoom.

Thoom.

Thoom.

Thoom.

Rezyl squinted against the dark as he slid new lead into his cannon's cylinder.

A shape took form, approaching from the deep.

A being of might and mass that dwarfed the Titan.

A cleaver the size of an ordinary man— bigger—hung effortlessly in its hand.

Its body was thick with ornate bone—a living armor that was one with the beast.

Rezyl let out an accepting sigh.

The creature walked like a man burdened by untold sin—lumbering and slow, though its stride covered ground with unnatural ease.

To Rezyl, the approaching horror cut an imposing silhouette not unlike that of an ancient, disgraced knight.

Maybe it had been heroic once.

Maybe here in these shadows, to the watchful eyes of the wicked woman and her rotting horde it was a hero still—only for a darker, sinister cause.

The thought intrigued Rezyl.

The fight he had come all this way to find, the enemy he had hoped was nothing but a legend's lie, seemed eager to greet him.

He smiled beneath his helm, then spun his Rose with a confident Hunter's twirl, before steadying his aim and fanning its hammer once more.

The angry bloom lit the dark.

Six shots, center mass.

Rezyl's lead pinged off a sudden, shimmering wall of black.

The knight had conjured a protective barrier as if from nothing.

Unable to comprehend the creature's arcane methods—dark magic or unimagined tech, or even a joining of the two, Rezyl didn't care. He reloaded and prepared to face the unknown.

As the ethereal shield faded the beast raised its blade and let loose an aggressive, inhuman roar: Hell's own battle cry.

Rezyl accepted the challenge.

His Rose gripped tightly in his vice grip, the Titan charged forward.

He would meet the shadow's rage head-on.

—

Two days had passed since Rezyl stepped from the dark corridors beneath the moon, back into the light. His Ghost pressed him for details time and again. He wanted to know all he could of the wicked woman and her promise of suffering.

Of the sea of mindless, chittering death.

Of the hulking knight and Rezyl's epic battle.

The Ghost was enthralled and deeply concerned. If the monsters below the moon were active and aware, the City must be warned. Rezyl agreed.

As they watched another Earth-rise from the lonely quiet of the lunar surface and planned their long journey home, Rezyl pulled fragmented bone from the pouch that hung on his left hip: a reminder of the evil that lurked beyond the light, and the last remnants of the wicked woman's betrothed.

And while he recounted once more the events of his time in the shadows he took his Rose from its holster and began grafting the bone to its steel frame—just another trophy, from another battle won.

—

It was only later, and far too late, that the first whispers came and the bones revealed their true, jagged purpose.

CHAPTER 3

Shadows Beyond

In the beginning, I toed the line.

My Ghost brought me up out of the long black, led me to a gun, told me I was a warrior. She said I was supposed to protect humanity. I told her I didn't see much reason in fighting for people who'd never given one damn about me.

She said I was special. I told her if that was true, she wouldn't have found my bones in the back-end of nowhere. Didn't know who I'd been before she woke me up, but I knew enough to know I was no hero.

Her rules didn't make much sense to me. I was supposed to do all the bleeding. All the dying. I was the one pulling the trigger. I was the one who couldn't close my eyes without seeing one of a thousand things I'd rather forget. Nightmares that turned into horrors on planets that weren't my own that turned into more nightmares.

The rest didn't have to do anything but be saved.

So I started thinking. Then I started reading. I'm no Warlock, but it didn't take a Warlock to track down the stories. Of the Risen who'd taken ahold of the Dark and made it his own. The man who'd gone down into the tunnels and burned down the horrors. Took their remains and wore them like a king. Stripped away the petals of the rose like broken shards.

They say he fell to corruption. That he lost himself and had to be put down. That the Man with the Golden Gun is the hero who saved the day.

I don't believe it. I'm not the only one, either—not many of us left now, but we've walked in his dust. We know everything he ever did. We understand what you don't.

He wasn't the demon the stories make him out to be. He was showing us the way.

My Ghost doesn't talk much these days. When she does, she calls me by my old name. Callum.

I don't answer to that anymore.

Blind Watch

A Rising Plague

SUBJECT: THREAT ASSESSMENT

PARTIES: Two [2]. One [1] Guardian-type, Class Warlock, Vanguard Designate [u.1]; One [1] Guardian-type, Class Titan [u.2]

ASSOCIATIONS: Blind Watch; Buried City; Cabal; Clovis Bray; Crucible; Exclusion Zone; Lord Shaxx; Mars; Meridian Bay [Mars]; Orsa, Zyre; Vanguard; Rey, Ikora; Thorn; Yor, Dredgen

//AUDIO UNAVAILABLE//

//TRANSCRIPT FOLLOWS.../

[u.1:01] I'm assuming you're aware of the events on Mars.

[u.2:01] The results from Blind Watch?

[u.1:02] Yes. It may be starting again. Not saying it is, but we need to keep an eye on any who would seek to retrace Yor's path.

[u.2:02] Agreed. But Orsa and his friends seem to have contained what Yor could not.

[u.1:03] A dangerous assumption. The Thorn's pestilence is becoming commonplace.

Widow's Court

Servants of Death

TYPE: POST-MATCH REPORT

PARTIES: Two [2]. One [1] Guardian-type, Class Hunter [u.1]; One [1] Guardian-type, Class Warlock, Vanguard Designate [u.2]

ASSOCIATIONS: Crucible; European Dead Zone; Fallen; Lord Shaxx; Malphur, Shin; Rey, Ikora; Thorn; Widow's Court

//AUDIO UNAVAILABLE//

//TRANSCRIPT FOLLOWS.../

[u.1:01]   I'm telling you this now, because you don't seem to be taking it seriously.

[u.2:01]   We are aware of—and share— your concerns and are monitoring. It could be you're too close to the situation to get a clear, full view.

[u.1:02]   Too close? I've seen the vids from Widow's Court. They're playing with death.

The Shadows of Yor

From the Journal of Teben Grey

They tried to hide the truth, but we've followed its winding path—pieced together the fragmented map of events across time and space.

Quite literally, mind you.

From Traveler's shadow to the dark corridors beneath the moon and the long, harrowing journey back again.

From the sickness inflicted upon the Crucible to the breaking of Light on the red sands.

From a forgotten settlement in the west to the horrors of North Channel and Velor.

From the wilds of the Breaklands to the hateful cold of Durga.

Finally, then, to Dwindler's Ridge, where Darkness met pure, angry fire.

We've traced Yor's steps from beginning to end and back again.

We've studied his reign—the terror he seeded, the violence he wrought as if free of conscience.

Only to discover a true and terrible thing: he was not simply the monster the legends claim him to be.

Though, in finding this truth, we've come to understand the desire to build an armor of false narrative around all he'd done—all he'd become.

Yet, that understanding—our understanding of the need to control Yor's mythology—should not be seen as agreement on the matter. Quite the opposite, actually.

When viewed as he truly was, not as he is imagined, we challenge the known mythologized depiction of the man who was Dredgen Yor.

In our estimation, the monster so many see was, in fact, the best of us.

His sacrifice total.

His vile means meant to carve a greater end.

They hide this truth because they fear the consequences of those who would dare follow in his footsteps.

To tempt the Darkness. To allow one's Light to be tainted.

Few could walk that ledge and not fall completely into despair.

And while theories exist to support or contradict the purity of the gift we wield, Yor's life offers a glimpse into unexplored possibility.

Orsa agrees.

He also believes, as I do, that there is a manner in which we may be able to replicate Yor's damnation while avoiding the same heavy toll.

We will surely be judged for what it is we are about to achieve. And there will surely come a time when the lone gunman will want words—or worse.

But we go now upon an old path.

One we seek to make our own.

And should we fail, may the Light avenge all those we make to suffer.

The Cauldron

Hateful Chrysalis

TYPE: POST-MATCH REPORT

PARTIES: One [1]. One [1] Guardian-type, Class Warlock [u.1]

ASSOCIATIONS: Cauldron, The; Crucible; Grey, Teben [AKA Bane, Dredgen]; Hive; Lord Shaxx; Moon [Earth]; Orsa, Zyre [AKA Vale, Dredgen]; Thorn; Yor, Shadows of

//AUDIO UNAVAILABLE//

//TRANSCRIPT FOLLOWS.../

[u.1:01]   We were facing a full squad. I recognized a couple of them—Orsa, Teben—but they were different. Decked out in dark gear and set to intimidate. I took it as an attempt at psychological warfare—up the creep factor in a creepy place. But it was more than that. They had changed.

Timekeeper

Unto the Abyss

TYPE: POST-MATCH REPORT

PARTIES: Two [2]. One [1] Guardian-type, Class Hunter [u.1]; One [1] Guardian-type, Class Titan [u.2]

ASSOCIATIONS: Crest; Crucible; Lord Shaxx; Orsa, Zyre [AKA Vale, Dredgen]; Supremacy; Timekeeper; Vale, Dredgen [AKA Orsa, Zyre]; Vex

//AUDIO UNAVAILABLE//

//TRANSCRIPT FOLLOWS.../

[u.1:01] Never seen anything like it. Orsa... or Vale. Whatever he calls himself. Coming out on top wasn't even in his plans. He'd just drop us then leave our Crests scattered around the combat zone. I don't think he collected one. Others didn't care. Figured it gave them a chance to pull the win. But I cared. Win or not, that kinda cocky ain't healthy.

[u.2:01] I don't think "cocky" is the right word.

Thorn 5
First, An Understanding

TYPE: Transcript

PARTIES: One [2]. One [1] Guardian-type, Class Hunter [u.1]

ASSOCIATIONS: Orsa, Zyre [AKA Vale, Dredgen]; Thorn; Vale, Dredgen [AKA Orsa, Zyre]; WoS, Yor, Dredgen; Yor, Shadows of

//AUDIO UNAVAILABLE//

//TRANSCRIPT FOLLOWS.../

[u.1:0.1] We have tamed the sickness. Broken it with unwilling sacrifice.

[silence]

[u.1:0.1] Now we claim our reward. Have you heard the whispers, brothers? Sister? The shadow speaks. All we have to do is listen. Its secrets are a gift. Its gift? Our evolution. The others misunderstand. We are the Weapons of Sorrow—living and free. The hated heroes of this broken age.

The Last Word 5

The Last Hunt

TYPE: Transcript.

DESCRIPTION: Conversation.

PARTIES: Two [2]. One [1] Ghost-type, designate [REDACTED] [u.1], One [1] Guardian-type, Class Hunter [u.2]

ASSOCIATIONS: Breaklands; Durga; Dwindler's Ridge; Last Word; Malphur, Shin; North Channel; Orsa, Zyre [AKA Vale, Dredgen]; Palamon; Thorn; Vale, Dredgen [AKA Orsa, Zyre]; Velor; Ward, Jaren; WoS; Yor, Dredgen; Yor, Shadows of

//AUDIO UNAVAILABLE//

//TRANSCRIPT FOLLOWS.../

[u.1:0.1] Will you fight them?

[u.2:0.1] The Shadows?

[u.1:0.2] Those who have taken up arms in the name of Yor.

[u.2:0.2] The hope is they are more careful than their inspiration.

[u.1:0.3] Do you believe that will make a difference?

[silence]

[u.2:0.3] No.

[u.1:0.4] Then what will you do?

[u.2:0.4] The Vanguard has an eye on...

[u.1:0.5] The Vanguard have their eyes on many things.

[u.2:0.5] I'm aware.

[u.1:0.6] Then what will you do?

[silence]

[u.2:0.6] What needs to be done.

Cathedral of Dusk

The Unconsidered Sin

TYPE: POST-MATCH REPORT

PARTIES: Two [2], One [1] Guardian-type, Class Titan [u.1]; One [1] Guardian-type, Class Hunter [u.2]

ASSOCIATIONS: Cathedral of Dusk; Crucible; Dreadnaught [Saturn]; Hive; Lord Shaxx; Oryx; Rings of Saturn; Saturn; Taken; Thorn; Vale, Dredgen [AKA Orsa, Zyre]; Yor, Dredgen

//AUDIO UNAVAILABLE//

//TRANSCRIPT FOLLOWS.../

[u.1:01] Thorn, huh?

[u.2:01] Freshly-crafted. You like?

[u.1:02] A little risky playing with something that's been known to kill Guardians, isn't it?

[u.2:02] Look where we are. Everything in the system's been known to kill Guardians.

[u.1:03] Sure. But there's facing trouble and there's asking for it.

[u.2:03] This isn't like the stories we've heard about Yor. Vale figured this out. Tamed it.

[u.1:04] Can you tame a sickness?

[u.2:04] Good question. Let's go pick a fight and find out.

CHAPTER 4

A Vacancy

Oryx: Defeated

— Listen —

Death is the last part of living
and life is learning to die
The song is the same as the singing
The last truth commands me
to eat all the light in the sky

I will go on forever. I will understand.

Dwell a moment on the weight of what you've done. Contemplate the story you just ended. Will you ever do anything that screams down the millennia? Will you ever hammer your will on the universe until it rings and rings and rings? Oryx was an awesome power. Show reverence.

All right. Enough. Enough. A vacancy has opened, hasn't it?

How interesting. How very interesting.

Do you ever pause, dear listener, to consider who benefits from all this heroism you commit? Do you ever look around you and feel the faintest chill? As if you are the tiny little ball bearing placed beneath a great mass, so that it might, if pushed, begin to roll?

You're a god yourself, now. You've consecrated yourself. Emulate me. Use your power to learn.

There are worse things to practice being.

King's Fall

Where are you going? No, wait, listen.

I was right, at first. In the ever-expanding Blighted-place, even Light must obey the sword-logic. Even you Guardians, you best and brightest of the dying dawn, you drew blood in honor of the Taken King. The Warpriest did his duty, and you did yours. Oryx was challenged, yes, but challenged in the way of the Hive, which is to say that challenge is worship—is challenge—is power. Sword-logic. You played your part well.

You were not supposed to touch the Light.

How did you find your way into the King's Cellars? How did you even recognize that benighted draught for what it was? Do you not know that the Hive pursue Light precisely for the purpose of devouring it with slavering jaws and slick greedy gulping throats? How did you take (or rather, un-Take) the Blighted Light that Oryx gathered to offer in sacrifice to Akka, and ignite it so that it burned and burned the Darkness?

It was barely Light anymore. But you took it. And when you took it, you did not keep it. You set it free.

You fools! You disastrous, bumbling squanderers! It's not right! Who now shall be First Navigator, Lord of Shapes, harrowed god, Taken King? Not you! You might have been Kings and Queens of the Deep! But you have toppled Oryx and you have not replaced him!

There must be a strongest one. It is the architecture of these spaces.

Why are you leaving?

Touch of Malice

"Let them feel every lash, every curse, every touch of malice that they first dealt to me."
—Eris Morn

"A weapon that draws upon the Hive's ravenous Darkness itself—a weapon that could turn back upon the Hive all the suffering they have inflicted upon us—it is done. I name it Touch of Malice, for it is naught but the Hive's own doing. Take it, Guardian, and remember that they had a choice… and now so do we."

TO EVERYONE WHO INSPIRED US, WHO SHARED OUR DREAM,
AND WHO WALKED WITH US ON THIS INCREDIBLE JOURNEY
—TO EVERY MEMBER OF THIS BRILLIANT COMMUNITY—
THANK YOU FOR BEING THE MOST IMPORTANT CHARACTERS
IN THE WORLDS WE BUILD.

DESTINY GRIMOIRE ANTHOLOGY, VOLUME I: DARK MIRROR

Bungie

Editor and Design:
Lorraine McLees

Art Direction and Cover Design:
Garrett Morlan

Illustrations:
Piotr Jabłoński

Additional Illustrations:
Ryan DeMita
Jesse van Dijk
Kekai Kotaki

Franchise Direction:
Christopher Barrett
Luke Smith

Narrative Director:
Sam Strachman

Grimoire Curator and Editor:
Eric Raab

"A Book of Sorrow" writer:
Seth Dickinson

"The Burden of Light" and
"Shadows Beyond" writer:
Jon Goff

"A Vacancy" writer:
Jill Scharr

Additional Writing / Curation:
Christine Thompson

Lore Curation and Advisor:
Matt Jones

Layout:
Keith Lowe

Production:
Chris Hausermann
Jon Sim

Graphic Design:
Zoe Brookes
Elliott Gray
Tim Hernandez

Legal:
Ondraus Jenkins
Michael Schneider

Director, Consumer Products:
Katie Lennox

Creative Director, Development:
James McQuillan

Based and built on the inspiring work
of the talented individuals at Bungie—
too numerous to note—who have each
contributed to these words in their own
unique and important ways.

www.bungie.net

Distributed in North America by ABRAMS, New York.

Library of Congress Cataloging-in-Publication Data available.

ISBN: 978-1-957721-00-2

11

Manufactured in China